"W

Lieutenant James T. Kirk asked, studying the arrogant, disrespectful Academy cadet who stood before him.

The cadet hesitated for a moment—a primitive and not unexpected reaction. "Mitchell, sir. Gary Mitchell."

Kirk assessed the cadet. "I'll see you in class, Mr. Mitchell."

The cadet looked at him, unable to conceal his confusion. "Class, sir?"

"That's right," Kirk told him. "Federation History."

The cadet tilted his head. "I think you're mistaken, sir. I'm in Commander Chiarello's Federation History class."

It was the lieutenant's turn to smile. . . . "You *were* in Commander Chiarello's class. Now you're in mine," he said. "I'm going to arrange for a transfer, Mr. Mitchell . . . so you and I can get better acquainted."

STAR TREK®

MY BROTHER'S KEEPER

BOOK ONE OF THREE

REPUBLIC

MICHAEL
JAN
FRIEDMAN

POCKET BOOKS
New York   London   Toronto   Sydney   Tokyo   Singapore

An *Original* Publication of POCKET BOOKS

POCKET BOOKS, a division of Simon & Schuster Inc.
1230 Avenue of the Americas, New York, NY 10020

This book is published by Pocket Books, a division of Simon & Schuster Inc., under exclusive license from Paramount Pictures.

ISBN: 0-671-01914-7

First Pocket Books printing January 1999

10 9 8 7 6 5 4 3 2 1

POCKET and colophon are registered trademarks of Simon & Schuster Inc.

Printed in the U.S.A.

For Mike, Paul, Mitch, Lee, Chuck, Laurence, Lou, Sandy, Alan and Len, who still don't know what beats what

REPUBLIC

Chapter One

JIM KIRK emerged from the entrance to the immense lithium-cracking station, the sight of Lee Kelso's corpse still mercilessly fresh in his mind, and took a look at the jumbled, gray landscape ahead of him.

Craggy peaks rose haphazardly like the uncut gems in some gargantuan crown, piercing the bloated underbelly of the blue-gray clouds. The wind howled as if in pain, carrying the dust and tang of a dozen different metal ores.

Gary was out there somewhere, the captain told himself. Dehner, too. And they were his responsibility.

His.

After all, it had been Kirk's decision a couple of days ago to try to penetrate the shimmering barrier at the edge of the galaxy—an attempt that had ended bluntly in failure. Worse, it had snuffed out the lives of nine crewmen, all but disabled the *Enterprise*'s engines, and turned two of his staff officers into living fireworks.

One was Gary Mitchell—a close friend since his Academy days who had saved Kirk's life more than once. The other was Elizabeth Dehner, a willowy young psychiatrist studying crew reactions under emergency conditions.

Little did Dehner know how big an emergency she would be privy to—the emergence of a being who could shut down every system on the ship as easily as he could shut down his own vital signs . . . the birth of a power so huge, so terrifying, it could choke the life from a populated world as easily as it had choked the breath from Kelso.

And now Dehner was out there among the rocks at Gary's mercy, his living, breathing pawn . . . or perhaps his chosen consort. Either way, the woman was in unspeakable danger.

Tucking his phaser rifle securely into the crook of his elbow, the captain left the protection of the station and set out across the sandy open area surrounding it. The wind whipped around him, driving dirt and loose debris into his face.

Kirk barely noticed. His mind was too focused on the monumental task ahead of him. *I could have avoided this,* he thought ruefully. *I should have seen it coming.* But it began so innocently. . . .

After their violent reaction to the energy barrier, both Gary and Dehner had been examined by Chief

Medical Officer Mark Piper, who determined that the victims had one thing in common—a talent for extrasensory perception. Dehner's esper rating had been an impressive 089, while Gary's had been even higher at 091.

A small difference, statistically speaking—but a difference nonetheless, judging by the results. While Dehner's vital signs showed no change after what she went through, the change in Gary was hard to ignore.

His eyes, for instance, went from brown to a startling, luminous silver. His voice took on an expansive, echoing quality from time to time. And he began reading at speeds even Spock could barely believe.

None of that constituted a reason to fear the man. After all, the captain had always trusted his friend implicitly, no matter what the stakes.

But there was something in Gary's attitude . . . an arrogance, a disdain for those around him . . . that put Kirk on his guard. That, and the unsettling computer logs of the *Valiant*, the last ship that tried to cross the barrier at the galaxy's edge.

Reports of queries about extrasensory perception, for instance. And, later, of a self-destruct order apparently given by the *Valiant*'s captain . . . who had to have been confronted with a truly staggering menace to even consider such a command.

But even then, the captain couldn't bring himself to believe that Gary presented that kind of menace. And Dehner had believed it even less.

I was a fool, Kirk mused. *A damned fool.*

As he reached the perimeter of the sandy area and entered the cleft between two towering crags, he shifted the weight of the phaser rifle in his arms. After the shrilling of the wind, it was quiet in the shelter of the rocks. Deadly quiet, he thought.

After all, Gary could be anywhere up ahead. Anywhere at all. Senses alert, the captain pressed on.

At least the others will be safe, he assured himself. Spock, Piper, Alden . . . none of them would perish like poor Kelso. Of course, if he had paid a little more attention to Spock's warnings, Kelso might still be alive . . . and Dehner might be safe on the *Enterprise* as well.

Kirk recalled what the Vulcan had said at the briefing—the one that seemed so long ago now. *Soon, we'll not only be useless to him, but actually an annoyance. In a month, he'll have as much in common with us as we'd have with a shipful of white mice.*

The captain hadn't wanted to hear it. He had lashed out—told Spock he needed recommendations, not vague warnings.

And his first officer had risen to the occasion. *Recommendation One: There's a planet a few light-days away from here. Delta Vega. It is the only possible way to get Mitchell off this ship.*

Kirk had balked at the idea, saying he wouldn't do it. He wouldn't strand his friend on an unpopulated planet, where even the ore ships only called every twenty years.

But Spock had persisted. *Then you have only one other choice. Kill Mitchell while you still can.*

The captain had rejected the option. He'd told the Vulcan to leave him the hell alone.

Again, Spock had refused to budge. *It is your only other choice—assuming you make it while you still have time.*

At least act like you've got a heart, Kirk had admonished him. *We're talking about Gary, Spock.*

The Vulcan had scowled. *The captain of the* Valiant *probably felt the same way,* he said ominously.

It was that reminder that had finally swayed Kirk. Taking a deep breath, he had placed duty over friendship—and authorized Spock to set a course for Delta Vega.

As he neared the end of his passage between the crags, the captain stopped and scanned the area ahead of him. There was no sign of Gary—or Dehner either, for that matter. Just a sandy shelf that angled upward into a higher range of rocks.

Cautiously, Kirk emerged from concealment—though he wasn't certain anything could hide him from what Gary had become, or shield him if Gary decided to put an end to him. Step by step, he made his way to the shelf. Then, still wary, he began to climb it.

Suddenly, a boulder in his path came loose and rolled down the rocky surface beside him. The captain stopped and looked around, his heart beating hard in his chest, his phaser rifle at the ready.

He couldn't see Gary anywhere, but he knew it was Gary who had sent the boulder tumbling. Kirk could hear Mitchell's laughter in the wind. He could see his friend's smile in the swirling of the dust up ahead of him.

Gary was mocking the captain, toying with him— letting him know that his approach hadn't gone without notice. And, perhaps, warning him. Telling him to go back if he knew what was good for him.

Gritting his teeth, Kirk went on anyway.

He recalled something Gary had said back on the *Enterprise*, while he sat there in his bed in Piper's sickbay. *It's like a man who's been blind all his life suddenly being given sight. Sometimes I feel there's nothing I couldn't do, in time. Some people think that makes me a monster . . . don't they, Jim?*

That was when the captain had realized that Gary could read their minds. He wondered if that was happening now—if his old friend was tracking Kirk's thoughts, maybe even finding amusement in them.

Not that it mattered. The captain had to find Dehner—to save her if he could. And beyond that, he had to destroy his old cohort, no matter what kind of power he held in his hands.

Again, he recalled Gary's words in sickbay. *I can sense mainly worry in you, Jim . . . the safety of your ship.*

Kirk had eyed his friend. *What would you do in my place?* he had inquired almost casually.

Gary had smiled. *Probably just what Mr. Spock is thinking now—kill me . . . while you can.*

There was no longer any need for pretense. With his last remark, Gary had torn away the veil.

Kirk had tried to get at Gary before he could bring his power to bear, but his friend had raised his hand and pierced the captain with a hideously painful energy charge. As Kirk faltered, Spock had launched himself at Gary as well—only to be hurled back by the same kind of charge.

Then Gary had revealed a bit more of himself. *I also know we're orbiting Delta Vega, Jim. I can't let you force me down there. I may not want to leave the ship . . . not yet. I may want another place.*

He had smiled to himself with the utmost confidence. *I'm not sure yet what kind of a world I can use.*

Dehner had looked at him. *Use?* she asked in a wavering voice.

Gary began to get up from his bed. *I don't understand it all yet. But if I keep growing, getting stronger . . . why, the things I could do . . . like maybe a god could do . . .*

Before he could finish, while he was still intent on his vision of the future, the captain had slammed his elbow into his friend's side. Then Spock hit him also, and Kirk sent him sprawling across the bed with a right hook.

Taking advantage of Gary's stunned condition, they had sedated him with a hypospray. Then, as quickly as they could, they had brought him to the transporter room and beamed down to the dilithium-cracking station.

Kelso and his team were already down there. The lieutenant had grimaced at the sight of Gary, his friend as well as Kirk's, being dragged through the entrance to the facility and imprisoned behind a forcefield. But if Kelso had had any objections, he had kept them to himself.

After all, he knew that Gary had become dangerous. Unfortunately, he didn't know how dangerous. None of them did—or Kelso might have survived to return to the ship.

Dragging his thoughts back to the present moment, the captain came to the end of his sandy incline and peered over its crest at a path that wound its way among the crags. Still no sign of his friend. But Gary was out there, an almost tangible presence in the landscape.

Kirk got to his feet and shifted the weight of his phaser rifle in his arms. It was a heavy piece of ordnance and it was getting heavier by the moment. But then, its inventors had never meant for it to be carried by hand over long distances.

It was Spock who had ordered the rifle beamed down, after he had seen Gary attempt to escape his energy-walled prison in the cracking station—and only grow stronger for the experience. But, of course, the weapon hadn't helped any of them.

As the captain, Spock, and Dehner had prepared to leave, Gary had called Kirk's name. *You should have killed me while you could,* he said. *Command and compassion are a fool's mixture.*

Then Gary had hit his friend with another energy charge, as if the powerful barrier between them hadn't even existed. This time, the charge hadn't just sent the captain reeling—it had short-circuited his brain, plunging him into a deep, swirling darkness.

When Kirk woke, he was looking up into Piper's face. Apparently, the chief medical officer had been knocked out as well, for a while. And so had Spock, who was lying on the floor, unconscious.

Gary was gone, of course. And so was Dehner.

Kelso's dead, Piper had said. *Strangled.*

That's when the captain had made the decision to go after Gary—alone. After all, it was his fault that his friend had gotten this far. If he'd acted sooner, taken less compassionate measures . . .

Kirk had gotten to his feet and wrested Spock's rifle from his senseless fingers. *When Mr. Spock recovers,* he had said, *you'll both transport up immediately to the* Enterprise . . . *where, if you've not received a signal from me in twelve hours, you'll proceed at maximum warp to the nearest Earth base—with my recommendation that this entire planet be subjected to a lethal concentration of neutron radiation.*

Then he had set out to hunt his friend down.

And now, perhaps an hour later, the captain was still doing that. His back against a cliff, the moan of the wind loud in his ears, he followed the path—knowing he had little chance of catching Gary by surprise, but intent on trying nonetheless.

When he ran out of cliff face, Kirk turned the corner and followed the path between two rocks that seemed to form a portal—an entranceway. It was then that he heard the voice.

Gary's voice, speaking in the confines of the captain's mind. But it wasn't antagonistic anymore. It was soothing, almost reassuring.

9

"Can you hear me, James? You cannot see me, I'm not there. You follow the right path, James . . . you'll come to me soon."

Kirk turned—and suddenly, Dehner was standing there in front of him, just a few paces away. And her eyes . . .

My god, the captain thought, his heart sinking in his chest. Her eyes were glowing just like Gary's.

Chapter Two

Kirk realized his mouth was hanging open. He closed it.

"Yes," the woman said—if she could still truly be called a woman. "It just took a little longer for it to happen to me."

Dehner approached him, one step at a time. Instinctively, Kirk backed off—then realized that was the wrong thing to do, the wrong tack to take with her. She was still as much like him as she was like Gary, caught for the moment between humanity and godhood.

The captain looked around for her partner, his rifle at the ready. But Gary wasn't anywhere to be seen. At least, not yet.

"You must help me," he told Dehner. He turned to her again. "Before it goes too far."

She smiled an almost blissful smile, speaking to him the way he might speak to a child. "What he's doing is right. For him . . . and me."

Kirk walked past her, alert for his true adversary. "And for humanity? You're still human—"

"No," Dehner protested. "I—"

"At least partly, you are!" he insisted. "Or you wouldn't be here talking to me." The captain walked away again, purposely turning his back on her— showing her he didn't fear her, didn't feel any barrier between them.

"Earth is really unimportant," she told him, obviously comfortable with what she was saying. "Before long, we'll be where it would've taken mankind millions of years of learning to rea—"

Kirk whirled on her, his blood pumping in his temples. "And what will Mitchell learn on getting there? Will he know what to do with his power? Will he acquire the wisdom—?"

Dehner turned her face away, declining to hear any of it. "Please," she said, "go back while you still can."

But the captain wasn't about to go back. "Did you hear him joke about compassion?" he asked. He looked to the heavens, half-expecting Gary to come sailing down from the blue-gray clouds overhead. "Above all," he insisted, "a god needs compassion!"

He could feel a tingling in the air. It thrilled through him the way a vibration might make its way through a tuning fork.

"Mitchell!" he bellowed, his voice tearing through the howl of the wind.

It was a challenge. But for now, it went unanswered.

Kirk turned to Dehner again. When he spoke to her, it was in a softer voice, a voice that pled for reason. "Elizabeth . . ."

"What do you know about gods?" she demanded haughtily.

"Then let's talk about humans," he said, making use of the opening she had given him. "Let's talk about our frailties. As powerful as he gets, he'll still have all that inside him."

Dehner looked away. "Go back!" she told him.

But the captain refused to be ignored. He grabbed her arm, eliciting a flash of anger from her.

"You were a psychiatrist once," he reminded her. "You know the ugly, savage things we all keep buried, that none of us dares expose. But he'll dare!"

Dehner didn't say anything. But she was wavering, if only a little bit. Kirk was getting somewhere.

"Who's to stop him?" he pressed. "He doesn't need to care! Be a psychiatrist for one minute longer. What do you see happening to him? What's your prognosis, Doctor?"

Suddenly, Dehner's look turned introspective. "He's coming," she said softly, less a warning than an observation.

The captain raised his rifle and looked around, his nerves stretched taut. "Then watch him," he instructed Dehner. "Hang on to being a human for one minute longer."

He had barely gotten the words out before he heard Gary's voice—not in his head, this time, but echoing mightily among the rocks: "I'm disappointed in you."

13

Did he mean he was disappointed in Kirk? Or in Dehner, the agent of his will? There wasn't any time to ponder the question.

Because a moment later, Gary appeared on a rocky ledge just a few meters away. His temples were gray, but not with advancd age. If anything, he exuded even more vitality than when the captain had seen him last.

Kirk rolled, came up in a kneeling position and fired his phaser rifle. The ruby red beam speared Gary in the chest.

But far from destroying him, it splashed off him harmlessly. Expressionless, seemingly unperturbed, Gary gestured . . . and the captain's rifle flew out of his hands.

Gary looked at Kirk with those ice-cold orbs that had replaced his eyes. "I'm contemplating the death of an old friend," he said. He glanced at a huge, misshapen boulder protruding from the cliff face in back of him. "He deserves a decent burial, at least."

The captain didn't have to think very hard to know which old friend his adversary was talking about.

Suddenly, Gary gestured and an open grave appeared in the sandy ground. He gestured again and a granite headstone materialized—with the name JAMES R. KIRK etched into it.

The captain got it. After all, Kirk's middle name was Tiberius. The "R" was an old joke between them—one of many.

Before he could say anything, Gary gestured again, projecting invisible beams of force at the boulder overhead. It started to tug loose from its moorings, dislodging dirt and debris. The rock teetered for a moment, as if it would fall—then hung there, defying the law of gravity.

"Stop it, Gary," cried Dehner.

Gary heard, but he didn't look at her. His strange, silver eyes were trained on the captain alone.

"Morals," he said reasonably, "are for men, not gods."

The captain got to his feet. "God," he said, mockingly, speaking of Gary instead of to him. "He's still driven by human frailty." He turned to Dehner. "Do you like what you see?"

She frowned.

Obviously, Gary didn't like being ignored. Again, he spoke in that expansive, echoing voice. "Time to pray, Captain. Praise me."

With a beckoning gesture, he drew Kirk stumbling toward him.

"Pray to *you?*" said the captain. "Not to *both* of you?"

Gary turned his palms downward, and Kirk felt a force crush him to his knees. He grunted with the pain.

"Pray that you die easily," said his former friend and colleague.

With another movement of his hands, he made the captain's hands come up in front of him. Kirk tried to move them, to no avail.

Out of the corner of his eye, he could catch a glimpse of Dehner's expression. She could see what was happening now—and the part of her that hadn't yet become godlike was horrified.

15

"There'll only be one of you in the end," the captain said.

Gary's fingers closed into a fist—slamming the palms of Kirk's hands together. Then he twisted his hand and Kirk's palms pressed even harder—so hard he could feel the edges of his bones grinding together.

The captain spoke through clenched teeth, enduring Gary's cruelty. "One . . . jealous . . . god," he grated. "If all this makes a god . . . or is it making you something else?"

His friend tilted his head, as if wondering how much pain Kirk could endure. "Your last chance, Kirk."

The captain knew what Gary wanted—what he needed. Validation—the confidence that he was all he felt he was. And, in Gary's mind, Kirk was the only one who could give him those things.

But the captain wouldn't do that—not even if Gary ground his hands to bloody stumps. "Do you like what you see?" he gasped, gazing at his tormentor because he had to, because he was forced to—but really speaking to Dehner. "Absolute power," he groaned, "corrupting absolutely."

Gary had obviously had enough. He raised his chin, probably pondering in what manner he should snuff out Kirk's life.

But before he could come to a decision, Dehner came to one instead. Raising her hands, she sent a stream of crackling, white energy at him, causing him to recoil and glow a livid shade of pink.

Then she did it again.

Gary shot her a look of surprise, which quickly

became anger—and sent the same kind of energy sizzling back at her. Dehner staggered under the brunt of it. He assaulted her a second time and a third, until her legs became weak and she sank to the ground.

But, to the captain's surprise, Dehner wasn't ready to admit defeat. She extended her hand again and fought back, sending another twisting shock through Gary's body. As he withstood it, his expression changed from anger to hurt—encouraging Dehner to attack him again.

He reeled, then pierced her with a charge of his own. It dropped her to her belly, but still she wouldn't give up. She seemed to sense that victory was in her grasp.

Her eyes narrowing, Dehner hurled the most violent surge of all at him. Gary fell against a rocky outcropping and slid to a sitting position. And as he sat there, a stricken, helpless look on his face, Dehner skewered him again and again with forks of deadly white energy.

Gradually, Gary changed. His temples lost their grayness. His expression became one of innocence, confusion. And the light in his eyes dimmed to nothing, leaving them very human and ordinary-looking.

Dehner's eyes had dimmed, too. "Hurry," she whispered, her strength clearly spent, her voice barely audible over the skirling of the wind. "You haven't . . . much time."

Kirk took her advice to heart. Advancing on Gary, who was trying to pick himself up, the captain snapped his friend's head back with a right to the jaw. Then he doubled Gary over with a left to the midsection and dealt him a two-handed blow across the back of his neck.

The captain tried to forget that he was pummeling his best buddy. He tried to tell himself that he was erasing an aberration, that this thing in front of him was no longer Gary Mitchell and never would be again.

But it wasn't easy. The face in front of him was his friend's, seemingly free of the bizarre energies that had turned him into something deadly and unimaginably powerful. The eyes that looked back at him with hurt and resentment were Gary's eyes, dark and undeniably human.

Somehow, Gary rolled to his feet. But Kirk was relentless. He planted his fist in his friend's belly, knocking the wind out of him. Then he chopped down on the bundle of nerves at the right of Gary's neck. When his friend didn't go down, the captain tried the same thing on the other side.

A normal man would have crumpled and blacked out. But mere seconds ago, Gary's body had been the vessel for enormous power. Some of it seemed to have lingered, fortifying him with more endurance than he had a right to.

Desperate to keep his adversary off-balance, Kirk threw Gary over his hip in the direction of the yawning grave. Somehow, Gary managed to avoid falling into the hole. But in the process, he lost his footing, sprawled, and slammed into the rocky ledge beyond it.

Diving across the grave, the captain leaped on Gary. But the man was far from vanquished. Scrambling to his feet, he knocked Kirk down with a shot to the jaw and staggered him again with a bludgeoning right.

Gary pulled his fist back for a third blow, but the captain blocked it. For a moment, the two of them grappled, each man seeking an advantage. Then Kirk saw an opening and capitalized on it, snapping his friend's head back with a hard shot to the jaw.

As Gary fell on his back, the captain leaped astride him, pinning him to the ground. At the same time, he caught sight of a rock about twice the size of his head—big enough, certainly, to splinter a man's skull.

Taking hold of it with both hands, Kirk lifted it as high over his head as he could. Then he looked into his friend's eyes . . . and paused.

"Gary," he said, "forgive me."

Then he brought the rock down, aiming for Gary's head.

But before he could accomplish his objective, his friend's hands shot out and stopped the rock from descending. The captain tried to force it downward, but he couldn't budge the thing even an inch.

Gary's strength was coming back—and quickly. Even as Kirk came to that horrific conclusion, he saw his friend's eyes begin to glow again with that weird, silver light.

The captain's heart sank. *I waited too long*, he thought. *And now it's too late—for everyone.*

After all, a being of Gary's abilities wouldn't allow himself to be marooned on Delta Vega. Not for long, anyway. He would find a way to escape the planet and return to Federation territory.

Before long, Gary would become ruler of all he surveyed—a despot who could annihilate any and all of his subjects with a wrinkling of his brow. Kirk bit his lip. Had any tyrant ever cared so little about life and death—or held its power so firmly in his hands?

Gary smiled up at him. It was a thin smile, devoid of humor or humanity. When he spoke, it was in a voice that seemed to be everywhere at once. "For a moment, James . . . but your moment is fading."

With frightening strength, he hurled both the captain and the boulder away from him. Kirk rolled as he hit the ground and got to his feet in the same motion. But if he'd expected a moment's respite, a moment to think, he didn't get it. Before he could take a breath, Gary was advancing on him.

The captain tried to gather his wits—to formulate a strategy. That's what he had been trained to do since his first days at the Academy. But what strategy could one pursue against a being of such unthinkable power?

Trying to buy some time for himself, he retreated to the far side of the open grave. But Gary followed him, one step at a time, obviously feeling no sense of urgency. He didn't even seem to notice Dehner as he walked by within inches of her.

Kirk moved away again and again, until he could feel the hard reality of the cliff face behind him. There was nowhere left to go, he realized. With his other options closed, the captain did the only thing he could do.

He struck Gary across the face.

Kirk had hoped it would catch his nemesis off guard. It did no such thing. With a tightening of the muscles around his mouth, Gary grabbed his friend by the arm and sent him flying.

Then Gary picked up a boulder no twenty men could have lifted, and—turning toward the captain—prepared to hurl it at him.

Why not? Kirk thought, trying to gather his feet under him. It had a certain justice to it, didn't it? He had attempted to crush Gary's skull with a rock, so his friend was returning the favor.

Gritting his teeth, the captain launched himself across the space between them. It was a move born of desperation. He didn't think he would actually accomplish anything with it.

But somehow, he managed to tackle Gary around the knees and make him stumble. And before he knew what had happened, they were tumbling into the open grave together, the boulder bounding harmlessly across the clearing.

Gary's mouth twisted as they disentangled themselves. No doubt, he was annoyed at the indignity of what had happened. He glared at Kirk, brought his hand up to send another bolt of energy at him . . .

But Kirk hadn't come this far to fall victim to his friend now. Somehow, he found the strength to duck the bolt, then leap out of the grave.

As he did so, he caught sight of his phaser rifle. It was only a few meters away, at the bottom of a rocky slope. Skittering down the incline, his heart banging frantically against his ribs, the captain grabbed for the barrel of the weapon.

Closed his fingers around it. Found the trigger.

And whirled.

At that moment, Gary was only beginning to climb out of the grave. His expression was nothing short of murderous—and to such a being, Kirk knew, there was hardly any difference between thought and deed.

But he had hit Gary with a phaser beam moments earlier, to no avail. What good would it do the captain to take another shot at him? He'd laugh it off and keep on coming.

Think, Kirk urged himself. *Think as if your life depended on it.*

Suddenly, he got an idea. Aiming his weapon at the irregularly shaped boulder that Gary had tampered with earlier, the captain pressed the rifle's trigger. As the ruby red phaser beam struck the hunk of rock, it blasted away whatever force or debris still supported it.

The boulder crashed earthward along the cliff face, shaking the very ground on which Kirk was kneeling. Nor was the captain the only one who felt the tremor. Alarmed by it, or perhaps merely distracted, Gary lost his hold on the edges of the grave and fell back inside.

As Kirk looked on, spellbound, the headstone with his name on it fell inside, too. Then the boulder—the one that Gary himself had carved from the naked rock—came down on top of the grave with thunderous force, seeming to crush everything inside it.

A cloud of dust rose around the boulder, like the

final, dying exhalation of a primitive god. Warily, the captain stared at it, ready to fire again at the slightest sign of movement.

But there wasn't any.

Panting, muscles aching from the intensity of his effort, the captain watched as the dust cloud was torn apart by the wind. He caressed the trigger of his rifle with his forefinger, half-expecting the boulder to explode in a million pieces and reveal Gary in his terrible glory.

But incredibly, miraculously, that didn't happen either. Nothing seemed to move beneath the boulder. Nothing at all.

Kirk raised himself up a little, hardly able to believe the evidence of his eyes. Could Gary have been destroyed? Was it even possible?

Little by little, he convinced himself that it was. Gradually, tentatively, he came to the amazing conclusion that Gary Mitchell was as dead as the stones that rose around him.

Then it hit him. His friend, Gary . . .

Gary was dead.

He had taken the life of a man he loved like a brother. He had killed a fellow officer who had saved his life over and over again, too many times for the captain to count.

But if that was so, the superhuman entity who had threatened the Federation had died as well. The civilized worlds Kirk had sworn to defend were safe again, never knowing how close they had come to becoming the playthings of a power-mad god.

Heaving a sigh, he made his way over to Dehner.

She was lying on her belly, still breathing, if only barely. He lowered himself to the ground so he could look into her eyes.

They were a miraculous shade of blue. The captain wondered why he hadn't noticed them before.

"I'm sorry," said Dehner.

There was no need for that. She had more than made up for her error. But Kirk didn't say that, because the woman didn't look as if she had long to live, and she seemed to want to say more.

"You can't know," Dehner moaned softly, "what it's like to . . . be almost a . . . god." Then her head slumped and her eyes closed, and the captain knew that she was dead, too.

He touched her shoulder, overcome with gratitude for all she had done—not only for him, but for the entire galaxy. Unfortunately, there was no longer any way he could tell her about it.

Taking a deep breath, he let it out and realized how much he hurt. His cheek was bleeding, his tunic was torn, and he had broken something in his hand. Settling back against a rocky upthrust, he set his rifle down, took out his communicator and flipped it open.

"Enterprise from Captain Kirk. Come in," he said, his voice as fatigued as the rest of him.

A moment later, he heard the welcome voice of his first officer. "This is the *Enterprise,"* Spock replied, just a hint of concern rippling the surface of his Vulcan calm. "Are you—?"

"I'll live," the captain told him.

"And Mitchell?" asked Spock.

Kirk glanced at the boulder that Gary had pried from the cliff face. He still couldn't believe what he had done . . . still couldn't believe the nightmare was over.

Or that another, more personal nightmare had begun.

"Gary Mitchell is dead," he replied evenly, despite the feeling that something had lodged itself in his throat. "Dr. Dehner, too." He paused. "She'd begun to change into a mutant herself."

The Vulcan didn't express grief or dismay. He simply asked, "Shall I see to it that you're beamed up?"

The captain glanced at his friend's grave. "Give me a couple of minutes," he said.

"Aye, sir," came the reply.

"Kirk out."

Feeling the weariness he had refused to acknowledge earlier, he walked over to the boulder covering Gary's grave and sat down beside it. Then, in the privacy of his mind, he repeated the information he had shared with Spock—forcing himself to believe it, to accept it.

Gary Mitchell is dead.

Chapter Three

Spock, who had occupied the captain's chair since his return to the *Enterprise* an hour or so earlier, surveyed the faces of the other officers manning the bridge.

Piper, the gray-haired chief medical officer. Scott, the talented engineer. Alden, the acting helmsman. Dezago, the communications officer. And, of course, the ever-present Yeoman Smith.

They had all heard Captain Kirk's brief report. They all knew that Commander Mitchell and Dr. Dehner had perished on Delta Vega, the barren planet the *Enterprise* had been orbiting for the last several hours.

The knowledge seemed to evoke mixed feelings in them. Feelings of regret, no doubt, for Mitchell and Dehner had been their comrades. But feelings of gratitude and relief as well, for Mitchell had been changing into something they could hardly comprehend.

And what did the report evoke in the Vulcan . . . who had spent his life denying his emotions, training himself in the severe and spartan disciplines of the great Surak? What did *he* feel about his colleagues' deaths?

He felt nothing at all, of course. But then, emotions served no practical purpose. They were stumbling blocks, as Spock's father had frequently taken pains to point out.

If you wish to embrace the truth, Sarek had told him, *find the cleanest, most direct path. That will be the one uncluttered with love and hate, the one free of jealousy, fear, and shame.*

The path of logic.

But just this once, the Vulcan wished that he could break with tradition. He wished he could feel what others were feeling. Not out of base curiosity or even scientific interest, but because he was the first officer on this vessel and he had sworn to help his captain any way he could.

That was what he had done the day before, when he recommended—in the strongest terms possible—that Kirk go to Delta Vega and abandon his friend there. That was what he had done when he ordered a phaser rifle beamed down to the lithium-cracking station, not long before Mitchell's escape.

And that was what he wished to do now. Simply put, he wished to serve his commanding officer. But, for the first time in his life, he wondered if he was equipped for the task.

Abruptly, Spock stood and glanced at Alden. "Lieutenant," he said, "you have the conn."

"Aye, sir," came Alden's reply.

Then the first officer turned to the chief medical officer. "You are with me, Dr. Piper."

Piper, a large-boned man with age spots on his hands, didn't say anything in response. He just nodded, no doubt preoccupied with the captain and his medical condition.

Together, Spock and his colleague entered the turbolift and headed for the transporter room.

When Kirk materialized on the *Enterprise*'s transporter platform, Spock and Piper were already there waiting for him.

The doctor winced at the sight of his commanding officer. The captain didn't blame him, either. With his shirt torn, his mouth bloodied, and his limbs stiff from his exertions, Kirk knew he looked a damned sight worse than he actually felt.

Piper shook his head. "Come on," he said in his gravelly voice. "I'm taking you to sickbay."

In the past, the captain had done his best to avoid that place. But this time, he didn't argue. He didn't have any fight left in him, his struggle with Gary having sapped the last of his strength.

"Whatever you say," he told the doctor in a hollow voice, a voice that still echoed with the horror of what he had seen and done.

As Kirk descended from the platform, his eyes met Spock's. If the Vulcan was concerned for the captain's welfare, he gave no indication if it. Rather, Spock seemed to study the human as if Kirk were some new life-form he had discovered under a microscope.

The captain wasn't surprised. Though Spock displayed no feelings of his own, the Vulcan often displayed a keen interest in the emotions of other species. And at that moment, Kirk's emotions were like a wound, raw and painful to the touch.

A part of him resented the scrutiny. Another time, he might have said something about it. But not this time.

Instead, he handed Spock his phaser rifle. The weapon was nicked and scratched in a couple of places, and it had a thick film of Delta Vegan dust on it, but the captain would never be more indebted to a piccc of ordnance in his life.

"Take care of it," he told his first officer.

Spock accepted the weapon, his gaze dark and probing. "As you wish, sir," he replied.

Nothing more than that. But then, what had Kirk expected? Even after serving under the captain for more than a year, the Vulcan had never discussed anything with him except matters of policy and ship's operation.

The closest they had come to any meaningful interaction was a three-dimensional chess game or two. And even those had been silent, almost solemn affairs, devoid of excitement or any other emotion.

"Thanks," Kirk told him.

"Captain . . ." said Piper.

"I'm coming," the captain assured him.

Leaving his first officer with the phaser rifle in his hands, Kirk accompanied Piper out of the the transporter room. The doors whispered open in front of them, granting them access to the passage outside.

It felt strange out there, somehow—strange and unfamiliar, the captain thought, though it had only been a few hours since he and Spock had dragged a sedated Gary through the corridor.

A few hours, Kirk echoed inwardly. *Just a few. But the world was different then, wasn't it? There wasn't any blood on my hands.*

Gary was alive.

Just then, a couple of crewmen turned a corner up ahead of him. As they walked past the captain, they looked at him with a mixture of concern and curiosity, and Kirk knew it wasn't just his physical condition the crewmen were concerned with.

No doubt, they had heard some things, and perhaps guessed at others. And now they were asking, if only with their eyes: Are you all right? Are you still the commanding officer we signed on with?

He nodded to them, refusing to give in to the heartsickness that threatened to overwhelm him, refusing to give in to the guilt. Looking relieved, the crewmen nodded back.

"Morning, sir."

"Morning," he replied.

And he walked on.

A few seconds later, Kirk and the doctor reached a turbolift. Piper tapped the pad set into the bulkhead and the duranium doors slid open to admit them. They went inside.

As the doors closed and the lift began to move, Piper turned to the captain. His eyes were a mirror on Kirk's pain.

"Jim . . . I know it couldn't have been easy for you," he said. "What you did down there, I mean. Mitchell was your friend."

Kirk looked at him for a moment. What the older man was really doing was asking if the captain wanted to talk about the tragedy on Delta Vega. After all, with Dr. Dehner gone, Piper was the closest thing to a psychiatrist on the ship.

Also, the doctor liked Kirk. That wasn't difficult to see. In the year or so Piper and the captain had served together, the doctor had often treated the younger man like a son.

But when it came to unloading such a terribly personal load of grief . . . Kirk just didn't feel close enough to the doctor to do that. In fact, he didn't feel close enough to *anyone* on the *Enterprise*.

"He was my friend," the captain echoed numbly, hoping that would suffice as an answer.

Piper considered the response. He seemed to sense Kirk's reluctance to discuss the matter—and he was too professional to press the issue.

"Mitchell was my friend, too," the doctor said at last, because he had to say *something*.

Then the doors opened and they exited the lift.

Spock stood at his science station, scanning the surface of Delta Vega with his sensor array—making sure that Gary Mitchell was as dead as Captain Kirk had indicated.

It wasn't that the Vulcan didn't trust the captain's powers of observation. Quite the contrary. However, none of them had ever encountered a being like Mitchell before. They didn't know if there was a possibility of his regenerating himself, now or even at some later date.

On the face of it, it seemed unlikely that Mitchell or anyone else could come back from the dead, Lazarus-like. But stranger events had taken place in the past, and would certainly take place in the future. In that context, Spock felt compelled to be as thorough as possible.

Abruptly, the turbolift doors slid aside. Looking up, the Vulcan saw the captain come out onto the bridge. His hand was wrapped in a soft cast, which would give his broken bones an opportunity to heal.

All faces turned to Kirk. The captain acknowledged them with a glance and settled into his empty center seat.

"Set a course for Starbase Thirty-Three," he said.

"Aye, sir," responded the navigator, making the necessary adjustments.

"Take us out of orbit, Mr. Alden."

The helmsman did as the captain ordered. At the same time, on the forward viewscreen, the curved, gray surface of Delta Vega swung down and away and, finally, out of sight.

Kirk frowned. With his good hand, he adjusted the recorder arm on his chair and activated it.

"Captain's log," he said, "stardate 1313.8. Add to official losses Dr. Elizabeth Dehner. Be it noted she gave her life in performance of her duty."

Intrigued, Spock walked over and stood at the captain's side. After all, he hadn't heard any of the details of Dehner's death.

"Lieutenant Commander Gary Mitchell," the captain continued, his voice dead and devoid of inflection, "same notation."

The Vulcan cocked an eyebrow, curious about the lack of information. Kirk appeared to notice.

"I want his service record to end that way," the human explained. "He didn't ask for what happened to him."

True, Spock thought, he hadn't. He had been a victim of his power every bit as much as Kelso or Dehner.

The captain turned to the viewscreen, where the stars were streaking by on all sides as they left Delta Vega behind at full impulse. The Vulcan scrutinized it, too.

As he had noted earlier, he wished to lend Captain Kirk some support in his time of tribulation. He wished to be helpful. However, as Spock had also noted earlier, he was ill equipped to perform such a service.

Kirk had said as much himself the day before, when they were arguing over their options with regard to Mitchell. *Will you try for one moment to feel?* the captain had demanded of him. *At least act like you've got a heart?*

Unfortunately, he couldn't do that. As a Vulcan, he enjoyed a great many talents and aptitudes, but the ability to empathize was very definitely not one of them.

33

Still, the first officer thought, in the name of duty . . . couldn't he *act* as if he could sympathize? Couldn't he assume that attitude, if only for Captain Kirk's sake?

Of course he could.

"I felt for him, too," Spock said suddenly of Mitchell.

The captain turned to him, a look of surprise on his face. Shock, almost. When he spoke, there was a spriteliness to his voice that the Vulcan hadn't heard since he came back from Delta Vega.

"I believe," Kirk remarked wonderingly, "there's some hope for you after all, Mr. Spock."

The Vulcan sensed that additional conversation was called for. Certainly, the captain's expression was an expectant one. However, Spock didn't know what to say—didn't know how to respond.

He wished he had thought out his action more fully. He wished he had been less impulsive in his desire to help. But what was done was done, the Vulcan thought. There was no taking it back now.

Logic dictated only one course of action. If Spock didn't know how further dialogue should proceed, he would simply refrain from responding at all.

Kirk's expression changed. He was disappointed, no doubt, by his first officer's silence. And the longer Spock remained that way, the more disappointed the captain seemed to become.

"Then again . . ." he breathed.

Kirk turned back to face the forward viewscreen, leaving the Vulcan with the sense that he had missed a window of opportunity . . . that he had failed Kirk just as surely as if he had lost the captain's molecules in the transporter buffer. Nor was it likely he would come across another such window any time in the near future.

Spock regretted the way the incident had turned out. Nonetheless, he was at a loss as to what else he might have said or done. He felt so uncomfortable in this area . . . so completely inadequate.

Frowning, defeated, the Vulcan left the vicinity of the captain's chair and returned to his science station.

Kirk sat in a chair in his quarters and stared at the empty monitor screen in front of him, just as he had stared at the damned thing for the last twenty-five minutes.

Suddenly, he leaned forward and tapped a pad in front of him, activating the workstation's recording mode. "Mr. and Mrs. Mitchell," he said, gazing at the screen as if he were looking at Gary's parents, "I'm afraid I've got some bad . . . some bad . . ."

He couldn't finish.

"Computer," he said, "erase that last message."

"The message has been erased," came the response.

The captain sighed and sat back in his chair, wondering how he was ever going to get through this. It was never easy to tell people that their loved one had died while in your care. When you knew them as he knew Gary's family, it was doubly difficult.

And when you yourself had been their child's executioner, it was pretty near impossible.

Not that anyone was requiring Kirk to do this. According to regulations, it wasn't his place to notify the deceased's next of kin—it was Starfleet Command's. He would have been well within his rights to let the brass do the dirty work.

But Gary hadn't just been his officer, his colleague. The man had been his best friend. His family deserved more than an official notice from an unfamiliar face on their home monitor.

Let's try it again, the captain told himself, finding new resolve. A second time, he sat forward in his chair and tapped the workstation pad, starting the recording function.

"Mr. and Mrs. Mitchell," he said, "I've got something terrible to tell you. Gary's . . . that is, he died in the course of a . . . a vital . . ."

Kirk cursed himself and shook his head. It was no use. Try as he might, he couldn't seem to find the words.

Abruptly, he heard a series of beeps—the signal that someone was standing in the corridor outside his door. He was relieved to have something else besides his message to deal with.

"Come in," he responded.

The doors slid aside, revealing Montgomery Scott. The *Enterprise*'s chief engineer was a spare, wiry man who somehow looked most comfortable when his face was pinched with effort or worry. It was pinched now, too, but with something else entirely.

"Sorry t' bother ye, sir," said Scott.

The captain dismissed the need for an apology with a wave of his hand. "That's all right, Scotty. I was just . . . well, never mind that. What can I do for you?"

"It's Kelso's funeral," said the engineer. "I made the arrangements, as ye asked. It's set for noon tomorrow."

Kirk nodded approvingly. "Good work."

"I did nae want t' make any assumptions," Scott remarked. "That is, with regard t' the service. But it's customary . . ."

The captain felt a pang. "You can count on me for a few words," he assured the engineer. "Lee Kelso was a fine man and an excellent officer. It's the least I can do for him."

Scott managed a smile, albeit a sad one. "Thank ye, sir. That was all, really. I guess I'll be goin' now."

Then he was gone, sliding out the door like a ghost. But then, the Scotsman had never been a man to mince words. He was as efficient a conversationalist as he was an engineer.

Kirk sat back in his chair, reminded that Gary wasn't the only friend and colleague whose loss he was mourning. Fortunately for the captain, Kelso had no family, no next of kin who needed to be informed of his death. The man had been orphaned at an early age, without brothers or sisters.

On the other hand, he'd had plenty of family on the *Enterprise,* plenty of people who loved and admired him, and basked in the warmth of his congenial and often antic company. Even without blood relatives, Kelso would find no lack of tears shed for his passing.

Kirk turned his attention back to his monitor screen. He still didn't know a good way to tell Gary's parents about his death. But then, maybe there *was* no good way.

"Computer," he said, "erase previous message."

"The message has been erased."

The captain leaned forward in his chair and composed himself. He took a deep breath. Then he tapped the pad and began.

"Mr. and Mrs. Mitchell, this is Jim. I wish with all my heart I didn't have to give you this news . . ."

And he went on from there.

Chapter Four

Kirk was in sickbay, sitting upright in a bed, the low throb of his biosensors the only sound in the room. There was a monitor held in front of him on an armlike mechanical extension, positioned conveniently so he could read the contents of its glare-free screen.

But the screen was doing something strange. The image on it was changing several times a second, displaying one scientific monograph after another with blinding speed.

And that wasn't the strangest thing—because as fast as the images on the screen changed, as fast as one monograph replaced another, Kirk was able to follow them without any trouble at all.

No, not just follow . . . absorb them. Understand

39

them. And even extrapolate on the data contained in them.

What was going on? he asked himself. What had happened to him? He reached for the control panel at the base of the monitor extension and made the screen in front of him go blank. In its sleek, rectangular darkness, he could see his own face now.

It looked different, somehow. Unfamiliar. Kirk leaned a bit closer and saw why. It was his eyes.

They were gleaming with a strange, silver light.

Something stiffened in him. He had seen eyes like those before. Before he could remember where, he heard the soft breath of air that signaled the opening of a door. Someone entered sickbay—and even before he turned to see who it was, he knew.

It was his friend, Gary Mitchell. *Captain* Gary Mitchell. Not only his pal since his Academy days, but his commanding officer as well.

"Gary," said Kirk.

"How are you feeling?" asked Mitchell.

"Something's happening to me," Kirk told him, his mouth dry and getting drier by the moment. "Something . . . bad, I think. I mean, I can do things I've never done before, but . . ." He swallowed. "Dammit, I'm scared."

Gary nodded grimly. "I know, Jim."

Kirk held his hand out. "You're my friend, for godsakes. You've got to help me," he pleaded.

But he wasn't speaking normally anymore. His voice had become so powerful, so expansive, it echoed from bulkhead to bulkhead like a roll of thunder in the heavens.

Kirk looked at his reflection in the monitor screen again, amazed. What was he, that he could speak with such a voice? What in the name of all the stars and planets was he becoming?

He turned to the captain again. "Gary . . . please . . ."

The captain bit his lip, clearly sharing his friend's pain. But he didn't take Kirk's outstretched hand.

"Listen," he said, "I didn't want to do this, Jim. You've got to believe that. If I'd had any choice at all . . ."

Kirk didn't understand. "What do you mean?" he asked, his voice deep and ponderous, breaking like waves off the walls around him.

Gary didn't answer the question. He just stood there with an apologetic expression on his face, as if he were saying he was sorry for something that hadn't happened yet.

Then, suddenly, he was gone.

In fact, all of sickbay was gone. Kirk found himself floating in the immense starlit vastness of space, his arms and legs flailing, his skin an agony of tiny, cold pinpricks. Cursing inwardly, he held his breath . . . or what was left of it.

He looked around and saw that he was a hundred meters or more from the familiar shape of the *Enterprise*. The ship glinted invitingly in the light of a distant sun, but Kirk had no means of propulsion . . . no way to reach it.

And he couldn't hold his breath forever—not even in his altered, more powerful state. He could survive unaided and unprotected for only a few minutes at the outside. Then he would die like any other human being.

But as he floated lazily in the void, he began to comprehend. He began to realize what he had seen in his friend's eyes: fear, bone-deep and profound, the kind that overrode all other emotions. But it wasn't for himself that Gary had been afraid. It was for his ship, his crew.

That was why Kirk had been beamed off the *Enterprise*. That was why he was drifting in the endless sea of space now, cut off from even the remotest hope of survival.

Because he had become a monster—a clear and immediate threat to the four hundred other men and women serving on the *Enterprise*. Because he had become a problem Gary hadn't dared to ignore— even if it meant sacrificing the life of his best buddy.

Kirk might have hated him for it. But he didn't. In fact, he respected his friend for what he had done. Gary was the captain, after all. It was his place to make the hard decisions.

If their roles had been reversed, if Kirk had been the captain, he would have made the same hard choice . . . the same reluctant sacrifice. At least, that was what he preferred to believe.

It was that last thought that occupied his mind as he began to asphyxiate in the vacuum of space. . . .

Suddenly, Kirk found himself sitting upright in his bed, bathed in a cold, sour sweat. He was gasping for breath, drawing it into his lungs in great, greedy, throat-searing mouthfuls.

It took him a moment to realize he wasn't suffocating in the numbing chill of space. He was in his quarters on the *Enterprise,* where air was in mercifully abundant supply.

Not space. Not a vacuum. His quarters . . . where he was safe.

Shaking his head to rid himself of the panic that had gripped him, Kirk remembered something else. Gary Mitchell wasn't the captain of the *Enterprise.* He never had been. Now that Gary was dead, he would never be the captain of any vessel.

He found that ineffably sad, all of a sudden. Regret washed over him like a cold, heavy surf. Gary would never be anything to anyone . . . except a memory, maybe. And it was his friend who had killed him.

His best buddy. Me.

Casting off his covers as if they were shackles, Kirk swung his legs out of bed. Then he sat there on the edge of it for a while, remembering what he had done and trying to come to grips with it.

He kept telling himself he'd had no choice. It was either Gary or the rest of Creation. In the dream, Gary had made the same decision, hadn't he? That's because it was the only decision he could have made. The only decision *anyone* could have made.

And yet, he thought.

And yet.

As first officer, Spock often took command of the *Enterprise* through the night—or at least, what the ship's computer called "night" as it sailed through the darkness of the void.

Like most nights, this had been a quiet one. The Vulcan had had time to contemplate the events of the previous day, to turn them over and over in his mind and inspect them from every angle.

But none of it had told him what he wished to know. Clearly, he had questions that couldn't be answered by any facet of his experience. Only by speaking to someone with more knowledge of the subject could he obtain the wisdom he sought.

Spock was trying to decide whom he might ask when he heard the lift doors open and admit someone to the bridge. Turning in his seat, he caught a glimpse of Yeoman Smith with a computer padd in her hand.

Smith was tall, blonde, blue-eyed . . . what humans would no doubt have called attractive. Also, thought the first officer, she was efficient. She did her job well, in his estimate.

"Mr. Spock?" the woman said as she drew alongside him.

He looked at her. "Yeoman?"

"I have a requisition from engineering," she told him. "Mr. Scott's asking for backup parts in case we run into another phenomenon like the one that crippled us the other day."

It wasn't likely that they would approach the edge of the galaxy again, knowing what they now knew about it. Still, the Vulcan accepted the padd and perused the list, which included a number of power-coupling components. It seemed to be in order. Besides, he mused, Mr. Scott wasn't in the habit of making frivolous requests.

Entering his officer's code, Spock authorized the requisition. Then he handed the padd back to Smith.

She nodded. "Thank you, sir." Then she turned to go.

That was when it occurred to the Vulcan that Smith might have the knowledge he was looking for. Certainly, it was worth finding out.

"Yeoman?" he said.

Smith looked back at him. "Yes, sir?"

He scanned the bridge, making sure no one was listening to their conversation. Fortunately, the few officers present at this hour were all occupied with their respective tasks.

"I have a question," Spock said at last.

The yeoman shrugged. "If I can help, sir . . ."

"I believe you can." He crafted his query carefully, so there would be no misunderstanding it. "I have noticed that when humans mourn the passing of a comrade, they extend verbal condolences to one another."

It took a moment for Smith to realize she was being asked for confirmation. "That's true," she told him.

"Vulcans do the same," he said, "albeit in a more detached manner. However, I sense there is more to human mourning procedures—something more subtle, perhaps—which I have been unable to identify."

"Something more," the yeoman echoed.

"That is correct."

She thought for a moment. "Well, one thing we do is share stories about the deceased. Uplifting stories, usually. It's our way, I suppose, of establishing him or her more firmly in our memories."

Spock nodded. Now that Smith mentioned it, he had observed that form of behavior since the deaths of Mitchell and Kelso.

"But beyond that," Smith went on, "I can't really think of anything significant. Mainly, I suppose, we just keep each other company until we get over the hardest parts."

"Keep each other . . . company?" he wondered.

"Uh-huh. Sit and listen to one another. Or sit and do nothing at all. Even then, it makes us feel better not to be alone."

The Vulcan cocked an eyebrow as he considered the idea. Among his people, solitude was something to be sought after, even treasured—most particularly at times when one was troubled.

"Fascinating," he said.

The yeoman smiled at him. "If you say so, sir. Can I give you a hand with anything else?"

Spock thought about it, then shook his head. "I do not believe so. You have been quite helpful already," he told her.

As Smith returned to the lift, padd in hand, the first officer thought some more about what she had said . . . and resolved to act on it.

His hair still soaking wet from his shower, a thick towel wrapped around his waist, Kirk padded out of his bathroom on bare feet and made his way into his bedroom.

The bracing, cold water had cleared away the cobwebs, but his eyes still hurt and he felt hollow from lack of sleep. Of course, he could have lain in bed a while longer, staring at the ceiling and trying to will himself into a dreamless limbo, but he hadn't found the prospect appealing.

Better to get the day on the road, he told himself. Attend to business. Try to take the next step in the rest of his life.

The captain looked around the room, taking stock of his surroundings with the dullness of a man whose mind hadn't caught up with his body. By the far wall, he noticed, a freshly laundered uniform hung from the metal framework where Yeoman Smith had placed it the night before.

He considered the brand-new pullover shirt for a moment—the gold fabric of command, the even brighter, glossier gold of the captain's bands on the sleeves and the soaring insignia on its left chest. There was no sign of the ragged holes he had torn in his uniform on Delta Vega, no indication of the blood he had spilled or the injuries he had suffered.

If he went by his neat, clean uniform alone, he might have imagined he had never been to Delta Vega . . . never tried to abandon Gary there, never been forced to murder his friend in the end.

But it *had* happened—all of it. His nightmare had been a reminder of that . . . as if he needed one. He had killed his friend and it would haunt him the rest of his days.

With that grim thought in mind, Kirk began to get dressed. First he pulled on the pants, then the shirt, then the socks and the boots that had been laid out beneath them.

He was sore and tender in a dozen places, and his hand was still stiff and swollen despite the medications Piper had pumped into it. Sighing, the captain snapped on his plastiform cast, knowing the doctor would take him to task for it if he didn't.

Normally, he used his dressing time to project what his day would be like—to remind himself of what destinations he might have to reach, what assignments he might have to carry out, what deadlines he might have to make. He visualized each hurdle, each step in the process, and formulated a plan to deal with it.

But not today.

Today, Kirk couldn't find the strength to think beyond the present moment. He would take his duties as commanding officer one at a time, setting aside anything that didn't require his immediate attention. He would lean on his command staff wherever he could, knowing he still had a good one, and hope that that would be enough.

Crossing to his workstation, he pulled up the previous night's log, which had been updated just a few minutes earlier. It had been an uneventful shift, the captain observed. Just the usual notations on celestial phenomena and the occasional course refinement.

Business as usual.

It was a good thing, Kirk remarked to himself. But in light of what he and his crew had been through the last few days, in light of their increasingly desperate struggle for survival . . . a report of normalcy couldn't help but seem a little bizarre.

They had destroyed a burgeoning god, after all. They had buried a force of nature. The stars should have been trembling, their planets crashing into one another in panic, the Milky Way crying out in pain and wonder.

But to Kirk's knowledge, nothing in the heavens had marked the death of Gary Mitchell. Only a log entry, and a brief one at that.

Sighing, he stored the file and brought up another one—the captain's log in which he had reported his friend's death. Though there was no one else in his quarters to hear it, he read the thing out loud: "Lieutenant Commander Gary Mitchell . . . same notation."

Kirk winced. *I'll have to work on it,* he told himself. *Elaborate a bit. After all, the man deserved it.*

Suddenly, he heard a familiar beeping sound. Turning to his door, he wondered who might be calling on him at this hour . . . who would have bothered to notice that he was awake enough to access the night log.

Obviously, the captain thought, someone who was damned eager to speak with him. Maybe Scotty again, hoping to iron out some last-minute detail in Kelso's funeral service?

"Come in," he said.

The door slid aside, revealing the tall, slender form of his first officer. Spock was standing with his hands clasped behind his back, his features as impassive as ever.

Kirk was shocked. The Vulcan had served as his

executive officer for more than a year to that point, yet he had never made an effort to visit the captain in his quarters.

Why the change of heart, Kirk wondered . . . if "heart" was a word that could even be applied to a Vulcan? Then he recalled Spock's comment on the bridge the day before.

"I felt for him, too," he had said.

The captain had been surprised then as well. He had even dared hope the Vulcan meant it. Then he had seen the expression on Spock's face—or rather, the lack of one—and had realized it was only a courtesy.

Just as the man's appearance now was, no doubt, merely a courtesy.

"Well," said Kirk, "don't just stand there."

Tentatively, the Vulcan stepped into the room. With a soft hiss, the door closed behind him.

"Is everything all right?" the captain asked him.

"It is," Spock confirmed, looking around. "For the moment, Lieutenant Alden has the conn."

Kirk waited for his first officer to say something more, but Spock just stood there. If there was a reason for his visit, he seemed reluctant—or even unable—to speak of it.

"Look," said the captain, "if there's something I can—"

"I would like to apologize," the Vulcan blurted.

Kirk regarded him. "Apologize?"

"Yes. Yesterday, on the bridge, I responded . . . inadequately to your emotional turmoil. I would like an opportunity to rectify that oversight."

The captain sat back in his chair. "I don't think I understand what you mean, Mr. Spock."

"When humans mourn, they require the company of their colleagues and . . ." The first officer stumbled slightly over the next word. ". . . friends. Yesterday, I saw you mourning the death of Commander Mitchell, but I failed to provide such company. I would like to do so now."

Kirk couldn't help smiling to himself. "I appreciate the thought, Spock, but it's really not necessary."

The first officer blinked. "Then you no longer experience sadness over the death of your friend?"

"I do," said the captain. "But that doesn't mean—"

"And would it not help you to discuss your feelings?"

Kirk sighed. "It would, I suppose. But—"

Spock cocked an eyebrow. "But I am not the individual with whom you wish to discuss them."

Inwardly, at least, the captain was about to agree— when he realized that, out of everyone left on the *Enterprise,* the Vulcan might well be the best friend left to him.

It came as something of a shock. After all, he really didn't know Spock very well. In most respects, the first officer kept to himself. But there had always been a bond of mutual respect between them. . . .

No, Kirk decided. It was more than that, somehow. He respected Piper, too, but he had no inclination to confide in the man.

So what made him feel more at home with Spock, despite the Vulcan's alienness? The captain looked inside himself for an answer and couldn't come up with one.

"Sir?" Spock prodded.

"Actually," said Kirk, "I'd as soon discuss them with you as with anyone. I'm just not sure I—"

"Tell me about Commander Mitchell," the Vulcan suggested.

The captain was caught off-balance. "Excuse me?"

"Commander Mitchell. Tell me about him."

Kirk could see that his first officer wasn't going to take no for an answer. And since he had more than an hour before his presence would be required on the bridge . . .

The captain gestured to a chair on the other side of the room. Obediently, Spock took it.

"What, specifically, did you want to know?" Kirk asked.

The Vulcan's eyes narrowed. "I served with Commander Mitchell for thirteen months and twelve days," he noted. "However, I never delved into his personal history . . . never learned a great deal about where he came from or how he became a Starfleet officer. I would appreciate it if you could correct those gaps in my knowledge. You were, after all, his friend."

Kirk grimaced. "Where he came from and how he became an officer . . . that's a tale and a half, Spock."

The Vulcan regarded him with what seemed like infinite patience. "I am not needed elsewhere," he replied.

The captain saw that Spock was serious. It left him little choice.

"All right," Kirk relented.

The memories seemed to well up of their own accord, good ones and bad, transporting him back to a kinder but no less complicated time. A time of opportunities and uncertainties, hopes and fears.

"It was like this . . ."

Chapter Five

EIGHTEEN-YEAR-OLD JIM KIRK proceeded down the echoing hallway to his new office, his arms so full of textbook tapes that the topmost nestled under his chin. Cadets of all stripes walked by on either side of him, trying not to stare—and staring anyway.

Of course, Kirk could have waited for campus security to bring him an antigrav cart, just like any other new professor. But then, he was different from other new professors.

While they were veterans of Starfleet, he was only eighteen years old. Whereas they had earned their ranks in the course of mission after mission and achievement after achievement, he had been given a lieutenancy based largely on his conduct during the negotiations that led to the peace of Anaxar, for which he won a medal and the praise of his commanding officer.

Of course, the Palm Leaf of Axanar was just icing on the cake. Throughout his freshman year, Kirk had displayed a willingness to work hard and excel. He had been described by at least one professor as "the best command candidate I've had in nearly a decade," and by another as "a young man with virtually unlimited potential."

Hence, the teaching position—and the eagerness that accompanied it. Kirk's predecessor had removed the last of his personal effects less than half an hour earlier, and the lieutenant was already moving in to claim his new office with all the determination of a Klingon commander seizing a planet.

Never mind that it required a trek all the way across campus, or that the office hadn't been cleaned yet by the buildings-and-grounds people. Kirk was propelled by unbridled enthusiasm.

It was only in the last few minutes that he had begun to regret that enthusiasm. The stack of tapes was heavy and unwieldy—so much so that the muscles in his arms were beginning to cramp. Kirk was starting to feel as if he might not make it all the way to his destination without dropping his materials on the floor.

He had an impulse to set his burden down, admit that he had been foolish to try to lug it so far, and call for a cart after all. No doubt, that would have been the sensible thing to do.

But Kirk couldn't exercise the sensible option. The Academy had placed great faith in him—not only to

share his knowledge and insights with his fellow
cadets, but to maintain his dignity among them. If he
fell short of completing his little expedition, the brass
would certainly hear of it.

And Kirk would be embarrassed.

His mouth twisted involuntarily. He hated being
embarrassed.

Lord knew, he had been caught red-faced often
enough the year before, when Finnegan was around to
plague him. The upperclassman had made his life at
the Academy a living hell.

But Finnegan had graduated—if only by the skin of
his teeth—and taken a position on a starship bound
for the Romulan border. At that very moment he was
light-years from Earth, probably too busy analyzing
sensor readings to think about the plebe he had
tortured at every turn.

This year, Kirk resolved, he would be embarrassed
no more. He would be cool, unflappable . . . the very
picture of composure.

Unless, of course, he spilled his tapes all over the
floor.

Just as he thought that, the lieutenant heard something—a gibe, followed by muted laughter. Glancing
to his left, he caught sight of a pair of first-year cadets
in black-and-gold Academy togs.

One of the cadets was tall and thin, with a long,
freckled face and an unruly thatch of red hair. The
other was of average build, with dark hair and eyes.
The second cadet had a certain look about him—a
cockiness, the lieutenant thought—that set him apart
from the other plebes.

It figured he would make that kind of remark.

Kirk stopped and addressed the man. "I beg your pardon?"

The cadet's expression turned sober. "Sir?"

"Did I hear you correctly?"

"That depends," said the cadet.

"On what?"

The cadet lifted his chin. "On what you heard, sir."

Kirk's arms ached like crazy, but he wasn't about to go until he had gotten some satisfaction. "What I heard," he said without inflection, "is that I look like a stack of books with legs."

The cadet's dark eyes twinkled. "That's correct, sir. I mean, yes, I said that. But then, you *do* look like a stack of books with legs." He shrugged, poker-faced. "No disrespect intended, of course."

"Of course," the lieutenant echoed. "Tell me . . . what's your name, Cadet?"

The man hesitated for a moment—a primitive and not unexpected reaction. "Mitchell, sir. Gary Mitchell."

Kirk assessed the cadet. "I'll see you in class, Mr. Mitchell."

The man looked at him, unable to conceal his confusion. "Class, sir?"

"That's right," Kirk told him. "Federation History."

The cadet tilted his head. "I think you're mistaken, sir. I'm in Commander Chiarello's Federation History class."

It was the lieutenant's turn to smile, despite the burning sensation in his arms. "You *were* in Commander Chiarello's class. Now you're in *mine*," he said. "I'm going to arrange for a transfer, Mr. Mitchell . . . so you and I can get better acquainted."

The man didn't seem to know how to respond. At last, he muttered, "Thank you, sir."

"The pleasure is all mine," Kirk assured him. "Before we're done, you may find that you've become a stack of books with legs, too."

Mitchell frowned ever so slightly.

"As you were," the lieutenant told him. Then he resumed his progress along the corridor, his muscles knotting painfully.

He listened intently to see if the plebe was inclined to utter any more remarks, now that he had his back turned. Fortunately for Mitchell, Kirk didn't hear any.

It was fortunate for Kirk as well. After all, his arms couldn't have taken any more conversation.

As it happened, he made it all the way inside the confines of his office before he couldn't stand it anymore—and the stack of tapes cascaded from his arms. "Thank you," he said to no one in particular, closing his eyes and reveling in the feeling of relief.

Letting the door slide closed behind him, the lieutenant plunked himself down in his chair. His arms hung in his lap, stiff and useless, but at least his ordeal was over.

It was only after the ache had begun to subside that Kirk turned to the workstation on his desk, brought up the roster of first-year cadets, and requested Mitchell's transfer.

* * *

REPUBLIC

Seventeen-year-old Gary Mitchell waited until the stuck-up lieutenant turned the corner. Then he glanced at Karl-Willem Brandhorst, his red-haired roommate and fellow plebe.

"What's his problem?" Mitchell wondered out loud.

"Don't you know who that is?" asked Brandhorst.

Mitchell shrugged. "Should I?"

"Does the name Kirk ring a bell? James T. Kirk?"

Mitchell shook his head. "Can't say it does, actually."

Brandhorst rolled his pale blue eyes. "Come on, Gary. Kirk's the biggest thing around here since Garth of Izar. Starfleet Command can't wait to shove him into a big, comfy captain's chair."

Mitchell studied the other cadet, wondering if Brandhorst was pulling his leg. Apparently, he wasn't.

"What's so great about him?" he asked.

The redhead grunted. "From what I've heard, just about everything. He's smarter than anybody they've seen in a long time. He works twice as hard as anyone else. And he's got this air about him, this . . . well, you saw it yourself. It's like he was born to command."

Mitchell pondered the information. "Well," he said finally, "he wasn't born to command *me.*"

Brandhorst looked at him. "If I were you, I'd belay that kind of talk. Kirk's already got his eye on you. The last thing you want to do is rub him the wrong way."

Mitchell laughed and slapped his red-haired companion on the back. "You know what, Karl? You've got to loosen up. You're taking all this Academy stuff way too seriously."

The other cadet frowned. "You'd better start taking it seriously, too, my friend, or they'll kick your sorry butt out of here. There's a list of a thousand candidates just itching to take your place."

Mitchell knew Brandhorst wasn't exaggerating. Getting into Starfleet Academy was the rarest of privileges. Only an infinitesimal percentage of those who took the exam ever qualified.

It wasn't that Mitchell wasn't pleased to be there, or that he discounted the advantages of a future in Starfleet. He wanted to see the stars as much as any of his fellow cadets, and he knew he had to get through the Academy if he hoped to do that.

He simply didn't feel compelled to worry much about his studies, or for that matter, his instructors' opinions of him. For as long as he could remember he had gotten by on the strength of what came naturally. He saw no reason to change his strategy now.

"Let 'em itch," Mitchell replied at last. "I'm here for the duration."

"I hope you're right," said Brandhorst.

"Bet the farm on it," his roommate assured him.

Kirk tapped a stud on his control board and the oversized screen behind him came alive, displaying a ninety-two-year-old sensor image of a sleek, silver-gray Romulan Bird-of-Prey.

The vessel was essentially a cylinder with a cigar-shaped nacelle aft of amidships on either side of it. Its underbelly bore the blue-green device of a proud, winged predator—presumably, one native to the skies of Romulus, though no one in the Federation had ever determined that for sure.

"This," the lieutenant said, turning to his amphitheater of a classroom and his class of twenty-two first-year cadets, "is the ship the Romulans used to wage war against the people of Earth. That war began in 2156 and continued until 2160, claiming tens of thousands of lives from both sides, and culminating in the decisive Terran victory at the Battle of Cheron."

His students studied the screen and the curious-looking vessel depicted on it. All except one of them, Kirk noticed.

Gary Mitchell had glanced at the image of the Romulan vessel when it first came up, but had shown little interest in the subject since. He seemed to prefer staring out the west-facing window at the cloud-strewn sky hanging over the Pacific.

"Phasers, disruptors, photon torpedoes . . . none of those technologies had been invented yet," the lieutenant pointed out. "Both sides had to resort to the use of atomic weapons, which seemed to blow up in their prefire chambers as often as they did anywhere else."

Mitchell, he saw, had begun inspecting his fingernails.

"A great deal," said Kirk, "is made of the fact that Earth's forces had warp-speed capability, while the Romulans had to rely on mere impulse engines. But if you think about it, that difference wasn't the overwhelming strategic advantage it appears to be." He paused. "Anyone care to explain why?"

A number of hands shot up. None of them were Mitchell's.

"Mr. Santangelo?" said the lieutenant.

Santangelo, a small fellow, spoke in a surprisingly deep, melodious voice. "Many of the battles took place within solar systems, where planetary gravity wells prohibited the use of faster-than-light travel."

"That's one reason," Kirk agreed. "And the other?" He eyed the students who had raised their hands. "Mr. Eisner?"

Eisner had a high forehead and jughandle ears. "As you mentioned, sir, both sides had primitive weapons. For anyone to even think of hitting anything, they had to engage the enemy at impulse speeds."

The lieutenant nodded. "Good job, both of you."

He touched his controls again and the image on the screen changed. Instead of a single Romulan vessel, it showed an entire fleet of them.

"At one point," Kirk told his class, "Romulan forces came close to Earth—a lot closer, in fact, than many people like to remember. That proximity, that sense of the wolf at our door, had a profound effect . . . not only on the population that had remained behind on the human homeworld, but on Earth's ships and their crews."

Every cadet in the room nodded as he or she tried to imagine what it had been like. Again, Mitchell was the sole exception. He was peering out the window again.

"What do you suppose their reactions might have been?" the lieutenant asked his students.

As before, he saw several hands go up. Predictably, Mitchell's wasn't one of them.

"Mr. Mitchell?" he said.

The cadet turned to him. If he was embarrassed or even surprised, he gave no indication of it. He just stared at Kirk with an almost eerie lack of expression on his face.

"Their reactions?" Mitchell echoed.

"That was the question," the lieutenant confirmed. "On Earth? Or among the defenders out in space?"

"Let's start with the defenders."

The cadet went on staring at Kirk. His brow creased a bit. "Something unexpected," he said at last. "Not fear . . . that's what one might be tempted to think. But the defenders weren't afraid. No . . . they became determined, like cornered animals. Having their backs against the wall just made them fight that much harder."

It was the lieutenant's turn to stare. "That's exactly right," he said, impressed by Mitchell's level of insight. "The crews on those ships fought like savages defending their caves. And before they knew it, they had begun to push the invaders back."

The cadet smiled, obviously pleased with himself.

Kirk didn't return the smile. Instead, he went on with his lesson. He spoke of what life was like on Earth during the war. He spoke of the battles on which the fortunes of the combatants pivoted. And he spoke of the Romulans themselves—or rather, what little had become known about them.

Of course, he posed questions along the way, to get his students thinking in ways they might not have thought before. And every time he believed he had caught Mitchell napping, he posed a more difficult question—one that required some serious reflection.

But the cadet fielded every one of those questions flawlessly. Before long, it became obvious to the lieutenant that Mitchell was more formidable than he seemed at a glance.

Eventually, the chimes sounded, signaling the end of Kirk's class. "I want you all to read Dandridge's accounts of the Battle of Cheron," he said, as his students saved their notes and picked up their padds. "We'll be looking at that in depth next time. Dismissed."

The cadets got up. Mitchell was the last to rise and the last to file past the lieutenant.

"Mr. Mitchell," Kirk said.

The plebe stopped. "Sir?"

"I'd like to talk with you for a moment."

"What about, sir?" Mitchell asked.

The lieutenant frowned. "This is just between you and me. Not upperclassman and underclassman, not teacher and student. Just you and me."

The cadet nodded. "I understand."

Kirk waited until the door hissed closed. Then he turned to Mitchell. "Tell me," he said. "How do you do it?"

"Do it?" the underclassman asked.

"How did you answer all those questions without batting an eyelash," the lieutenant asked, "when it's clear you're not the least bit interested in the subject matter?"

Mitchell smiled a cryptic smile, piquing Kirk's curiosity even more. "You won't hold it against me, sir?"

"You have my word," said the upperclassman.

The plebe shrugged. "I just get these . . . flashes of insight, I guess you'd call them. I've gotten them all my life."

"Flashes of insight?" Kirk wondered. "You mean you can tell what's going on in my head?"

"No," said Mitchell. "It's not that black-and-white. But I can tell how you feel about something. And most of the time, I can put that together with some other cue and come up with a picture."

Growing up in Iowa, Kirk had heard about such people. He had just never run into one himself.

"I'm no Vulcan, mind you," said Mitchell. "But, more often than not, I can figure out what people are thinking."

The lieutenant wanted a demonstration. "All right, then," he said. "What am I thinking right now?"

The cadet examined Kirk's expression. "You're thinking I'm only half the jerk you figured me for."

The upperclassman realized his mouth was hanging open. With a conscious effort, he closed it.

"Pretty close?" Mitchell asked.

"Pretty close," Kirk conceded.

"That's a big reason I got into the Academy," the cadet admitted. "I mean, I wasn't exactly a model student in other ways. But when it came to figuring things out . . . figuring people out, I should say . . . I've always been among the crème de la crème."

The lieutenant shook his head. "But you study, too," he insisted, refusing to believe the contrary.

The plebe shrugged. "I study the things I feel like studying. Warp-engine design, for instance. And stellar navigation. I can't get enough of that stuff. But when it comes to history, philosophy, comparative sociology . . . I get bored pretty easily."

Kirk winced at the admission. In all the time he had been at the Academy, he had never heard anyone say anything like that.

Also, he didn't know how he felt about the idea of someone getting by on intuition alone. It didn't seem fair to the other cadets.

"I know," said Mitchell. "You think what I do is cheating, in a way. You think I should step aside and give my spot to some more deserving person—someone who fits the mold a little better."

The lieutenant felt himself go red in the face. "I didn't say that," he responded defensively.

"You didn't have to," Mitchell reminded him. "Flashes of insight, remember?"

Kirk frowned. "All right," he conceded. "Maybe I do think the opportunity might be appreciated more by someone else."

"Then you'd be wrong," said Mitchell. "Nobody wants to get to the stars more than I do."

The upperclassman fixed him with his gaze. "And you think you're going to get there with parlor tricks?"

The cadet stiffened a little. "Are you telling me

intuition isn't valuable, Lieutenant? Or that it wouldn't go a long way toward understanding a species we've never encountered before?"

Kirk couldn't say that. For all he knew, it might be an asset at that. But it didn't seem right that Mitchell should get by while his fellow plebes studied their tails off.

"I ought to be getting to my next class," said the cadet.

Unable to carry his protest any further, the lieutenant nodded. "You're dismissed, Mr. Mitchell."

The younger man looked at him. "And you won't spread this around? My having this talent, I mean?"

Kirk wished he could. "As I said, you have my word on it."

"Good. I'll see you tomorrow . . . sir." And with that, the cadet left the lieutenant's classroom.

Kirk stood there for a moment, resenting Mitchell on behalf of everyone who ever stayed up half the night trying to master a first-year curriculum. But he had to admit he envied the man a little, too.

After all, Mitchell did seem to understand people, and that was an area where the lieutenant still needed some work.

Chapter Six

GARY MITCHELL was lying on his bed in his underwear, going over the day's events in his mind as he tossed a blue rubber racquetball in the air. Catching the ball on its way down, he said, "I'm not bothering you, am I?"

Gangly Karl-Willem Brandhorst, who was bent over his desk on the other side of the room, grunted and shot a glance at him. "And if you were?"

Mitchell shrugged. "I guess I'd find some other place to pass the time. Of course, I'd be hard-pressed to say where that might be. The Academy isn't exactly a hotbed of sensory stimuli at this time of night."

"For good reason," said his roommate. "Most people are studying. And those who aren't, are asleep."

Mitchell tossed the ball in the air again and caught

it. "You know," he mused out loud, "Kirk got me thinking today."

Brandhorst feigned surprise. "You think? I mean, in addition to all your other amazing talents?"

The other cadet smiled to himself, unoffended. "I wouldn't have admitted it to the lieutenant, mind you, but his lesson wasn't the most boring thing I'd ever heard. There were a few moments there when I actually found myself listening to him."

Brandhorst grunted. "That's quite a compliment, coming from you."

"Yeah," said Mitchell, acknowledging the truth of the remark. "It is a compliment, isn't it?"

He launched the racquetball at the ceiling, trying to see how close he could come without hitting it. The ball peaked within a few inches of the smooth, white surface before gravity claimed it and brought it plummeting back to earth.

Then Mitchell's mind switched tracks. "You say Lieutenant Kirk is the fair-haired boy around here?" he asked.

"That's what they tell me," said Brandhorst.

"There's something about him, all right," Mitchell agreed, considering the various aspects of the lieutenant's personality the way someone else might consider the facets of a diamond or the electron orbits in a duranium molecule. "Something different, y'know? The man could go places . . . providing he gets some assistance from the right people, of course."

The redhead looked at him. "Pardon me for asking . . . but what the devil are you talking about?"

Mitchell propelled the ball upward and watched it

come within a hairsbreadth of the ceiling. Then, with a flick of his wrist, he snatched it out of the air on its way down.

"I mean," he said, "Kirk's in a funny position here. He's too young to be friendly with the other professors and too hoity-toity to rub elbows with his fellow cadets."

"So?" Brandhorst prodded.

"So I'm going to take the guy under my wing," Mitchell replied matter-of-factly. "I'm going to make him my personal project."

His roommate rolled his eyes and returned to his studies. "You—a first-year cadet who can barely find his boots in the morning—you are going to take a lieutenant under your wing? A man who's been earmarked for command?"

Mitchell shrugged. "That's what I said, wasn't it?"

Brandhorst sighed. "Honestly, Gary . . . sometimes I don't know what planet you're on."

Mitchell glanced at him with a straight face. "Gee, Karl-Willem. Maybe you need to study a little harder."

Then, having laid out his course of action, he balanced the ball on his navel and went to sleep.

Kirk scooped some white chalk powder out of the tray in front of him, rubbed it into his palms, and assumed a position beneath the gym's stainless-steel horizontal bar. Jumping up, he caught the bar in his hands and felt his weight make a statement in his shoulder joints.

His arms were still sore from carrying all his tapes the day before, but not so sore that they'd hold him back in his exercise regimen. Besides, it felt good to stretch out, to expand every muscle in his body from his fingertips to his groin.

For a moment, the lieutenant just hung there, taking in deep breaths to fortify himself against the considerable rigors that awaited him. Then he kicked out and began swinging from the waist, gently at first, but with ever-increasing authority.

On his fourth swing, Kirk brought his legs in closer to his body and slipped them over the bar. A single dizzy moment later, he came to rest with his hips against the unyielding steel. Checking his grip, he took a couple more deep breaths and rolled his body forward into a somersault.

That got him swinging again. He swung back and forth with considerable grace, finally reaching an almost vertical position on his backswing. When he came forward, it was with all the force he could muster.

Finally, at the apex of his swing, he let go of the bar and tucked his knees into his chest. He could feel the gym spinning around him . . . once, twice, and then a third time, his blood pounding in his ears.

As soon as he felt he had completed the third flip, the lieutenant unfolded his legs, keeping his knees bent only slightly. A fraction of a second later, his arms outstretched for balance, he felt the jolt of something solid beneath his heels.

Then his senses stabilized and he saw he was

standing on one of the gym mats, the stainless-steel form of the exercise apparatus a meter or so behind him. He grinned and coiled his fingers into fists.

Yes, he thought.

It was the first time he had ever executed the triple flip. He wished his brother, Sam, had seen it. He wished—

Abruptly, a sixth sense told Kirk he wasn't alone in the room. Whirling, he caught sight of two of his fellow educators standing in the open doorway. One was Mayhar-Perth, the xenobiologist. The other was Aaronson, who taught third-year subspace mechanics.

Both of them considered the lieutenant for a second. Then they turned and went back the way they had come, though their garb was a clear indication that they had planned to use the gym.

Kirk sighed. The year before, Aaronson and Mayhar-Perth wouldn't have left. They would have come in and used the parallel bars or the pommel horse, and in the process they would have shared some funny stories with him—even though he was a cadet and they were his instructors.

But then, that was *before* he had seen fit to rat on Ben Finney.

Mitchell was eating lunch with Brandhorst and a couple of their first-year colleagues, trading stories about their various classes, when Kirk walked into the mess hall.

The lieutenant got a tray full of food from one of the slots. Then, scanning the place with a glance, he frowned slightly and took a seat by himself in a corner of the room. As he started to eat, he kept his eyes fixed on the contents of his tray.

One of the other cadets sitting with Mitchell—a guy named Covaleski—shook his head. "Serves him right, I'd say."

Mitchell looked at him. "Who? Kirk?"

"That's right."

"Serves him right for what?" Brandhorst inquired.

Covaleski smiled a grim smile. "For what happened on the *Republic.*"

"I guess you haven't heard," said Chan, the fourth diner at their table.

Mitchell glanced at Brandhorst, whom he trusted to monitor all Academy gossip. "Do you know what these guys are talking about?"

Brandhorst shook his head. "Not a clue. Does this have anything to do with the Battle of Axanar?"

"Not even close," said Covaleski. "That was later." He leaned in a little closer to his fellow cadets. "Every year, we get to board a starship for a training mission somewhere in the Federation. The *Republic* is one of the ships designated as a training vessel."

"Okay," said Mitchell. "That much, even I've heard. But what's this got to do with Kirk?"

Chan leaned closer, too. "Last year, he went on a couple of those missions. The ship he went on was the *Republic.* And one of the instructors that went with him was a guy named Ben Finney."

The name didn't sound familiar to Mitchell. "Should I know him?" he asked.

"Kirk knew him," said Covaleski. "He and Finney had gotten to be friends. You see, Finney was the

73

youngest instructor here and Kirk was some kind of prodigy. They just hit it off."

"Anyway," said Chan, "the two of them were on the *Republic*, and Finney drew the first night watch. Kirk was scheduled to take the second one. But when Kirk came around to relieve his pal, he found a circuit open to the *Republic*'s impulse drive."

Mitchell didn't know much about impulse engines, but an open circuit sounded pretty dangerous. Chan's expression confirmed it.

"If it wasn't closed in time," said Covaleski, "it could have blown up the ship. So Kirk closed it."

"What's the matter with that?" asked Brandhorst.

"Nothing," Covaleski replied. "Except Kirk didn't stop there. He reported the incident to the captain."

Chan nodded. "Regardless of how it made Finney look—in other words, pretty bad. As it turned out, Finney drew a reprimand for it. And even worse, he was moved to the bottom of the promotion list."

Covaleski eyed Kirk across the room. "That's what the good lieutenant did to a friend—a guy he liked. You can imagine what he might do to someone he couldn't stand."

"And that's why the other instructors steer clear of him," Chan explained. He smiled. "Finney, in particular."

Mitchell regarded Kirk as well. "I see."

He had imagined it was just Kirk's age that kept him from fraternizing with the other instructors. Now he knew the truth of the matter.

Chan got to his feet and picked up his tray. "I've got to get going. Stellar cartography awaits."

"Me, too," said Covaleski, rising alongside the other cadet. "What about you guys?"

Brandhorst announced that he was heading to study hall. Apparently, he still had some reading to do before his metallurgy class.

Only Mitchell decided to remain there in the mess hall. After all, he had something to say to the erstwhile James T. Kirk, and he wanted to say it man-to-man.

Fortunately for Mitchell, it didn't take the lieutenant long to eat his meal. Without anyone to talk to, he didn't seem eager to linger. Minutes after he had come in, he was done.

Mitchell watched Kirk take his tray to the proper receptacle and insert it. Then, brushing his hands off, the lieutenant made his exit.

A few of the instructors looked up to watch him go, but none of them said anything. They just exchanged meaningful glances. A moment later, they returned to whatever they had been discussing.

That's when Mitchell got up, took care of his tray as Kirk had, and exited the room. He moved quickly, so the lieutenant wouldn't get too big a head start. After all, the Academy building was a honeycomb of corridors and he didn't want to lose sight of his objective.

Kirk was turning a distant corner as Mitchell emerged from the mess hall. Seeing that, the cadet broke into a jog in an effort to catch up with the lieutenant. He was starting to gain on his quarry as he came swinging around the corner.

That's when he felt something slam into his face with the force of a phaser set on heavy stun.

Unprepared for the impact, Mitchell saw everything go dark for a second or two. His knees buckled and a metallic taste filled his mouth. When his head cleared, he found himself sitting on the floor, his legs splayed out in front of him.

A steely-eyed Kirk was standing over him, his lips pressed together in a straight, angry line. The upperclassman was holding his right hand, the knuckles of which looked chafed and raw—as if he had just used them on an unsuspecting fellow cadet.

Mitchell nodded appreciatively as he propped himself up on one arm. "Nice shot," he conceded, wiping blood from his mouth with the back of his hand as he gathered his legs beneath him.

Then he launched himself at the upperclassman with a quickness that had served him well on the streets of his hometown. This time, it was Kirk who was caught unaware.

The two men went down in a tangle of arms and legs. Mitchell drew back his fist and got in a resounding shot to Kirk's jaw. Then another. But as it turned out, the lieutenant was no pushover. As he and Mitchell rolled on the floor, he got some leverage somehow and wound up on top.

"All right," he rasped, grabbing a piece of Mitchell's shirt with one hand while making a white-knuckled fist with the other. "Suppose you tell me why you're stalking me."

Mitchell looked at the upperclassman disbelievingly—then burst out laughing. And why not? It was the funniest thing he had heard since he'd arrived at the Academy.

"Stalking you?" he echoed. "You've got to be kidding. I just wanted to catch up with you. To talk to you."

Kirk's eyes narrowed. "About what?"

"About Ben Finney," Mitchell replied. "And the way you reported him for not noticing that open circuit."

The lieutenant's face darkened with anger and embarrassment. "I didn't exactly enjoy that."

"Of course you didn't," the underclassman told him. "That's the whole point. Finney was your friend, but you turned him in anyway. All I'm saying is it took some guts."

Clearly, Kirk hadn't expected to hear that. He let go of Mitchell's shirt and got off him. Then, after a moment's hesitation, the lieutenant reached down and helped Mitchell to his feet.

"Thanks," said the plebe. He wiped his mouth again. "They teach you how to fight that way in Nebraska?"

Kirk looked at him. "Iowa. But how—?"

Mitchell shrugged. "It's that ruddy-cheeked, farm-boy look. Iowa would have been my second guess."

The lieutenant's eyes narrowed. "Not bad," he said begrudgingly.

"I told you so. Now you guess. Tell me where I'm from."

Kirk shook his head. "I'm not the one with the intuition."

"Guess," Mitchell told him.

The lieutenant shrugged. "Chicago. Or Detroit."

"New York. Close enough. You got the big-city part." Mitchell pulled down on the front of his shirt to straighten it. "City mouse, country mouse . . . so I guess it's up to me to broaden your horizons, right?"

The lieutenant gazed at him as if he had grown another set of ears. "Broaden my horizons . . . ?" he asked.

"Uh-huh. And believe me, you need it."

Kirk looked at him askance. "If you don't mind my asking . . . what the hell are you talking about?"

"You've obviously grown up much too sheltered, Lieutenant. You need to loosen the reins, let your hair down, take a few chances. And you know what? I'm just the guy to show you how."

Suddenly, Kirk's attitude changed—as if he had suddenly remembered who he was and whom he was talking to. When he spoke, his voice resounded with the timbre of command.

"Listen," he said, "I appreciate the sentiment, Cadet—but it's misplaced, to say the least. If anyone's going to give any lessons around here, it'll be me. Understand?"

Mitchell managed a smile. "Aye, sir."

"I'm the teacher," Kirk reminded him. "You're the student."

"Absolutely. Whatever you say, sir."

"You'd do well to remember that," said Kirk.

"I'll do my best," the plebe promised him, though he didn't mean a single word of it.

Kirk spent another moment trying to figure Mitchell out. He didn't seem to get anywhere. But then, the underclassman thought, better men than the lieutenant had tried and failed in that regard.

"See you in class," Kirk said finally.

"In class," Mitchell echoed. "Aye, sir."

Frowning, the lieutenant walked away.

Apparently, Mitchell mused, Kirk was wrapped a little tighter than he had anticipated. Taking the Iowan under his wing wasn't going to be as easy as it had looked.

But that was all right. There was nothing Mitchell liked better than a challenge.

Chapter Seven

KIRK WAS halfway along the corridor when he realized what kind of ridiculous, boneheaded stunt he had pulled. All Mitchell had wanted to do was pat him on the back a little.

And how had he, the coolheaded upperclassman, responded in his infinite wisdom? How had he rewarded the plebe's sincere and spontaneous expression of admiration?

He'd belted the guy.

Nice going, Kirk told himself. *That'll look great on your record. "Command candidate assaults unsuspecting underclassman in Academy building for no good reason whatsoever."*

But in the end, it wasn't the lieutenant's record that sent him back down the corridor in search of the other cadet. It was his conscience. He owed the younger man an apology and he was damned well going to give him one.

As he prowled the hallways in search of Mitchell, Kirk drew stares from cadets and instructors alike. After all, he had at least one obvious and painful bruise developing on his face, and probably a few less noticeable ones to go with it.

Kirk sighed. Why did these things always manage to happen to him? As outstanding as his academic progress had been, as much as he had impressed the commandant with his actions at Axanar, his handling of relationships at the Academy had been a dismal failure.

Every step of the way, he had tried to do what seemed right to him. He had tried to act fairly and responsibly. And what had it earned him? In the case of Ben Finney, the loss of a friend.

And in the case of Finnegan . . .

Suddenly, he caught sight of Mitchell. The plebe was leaving the building through one of its several exit doors, which had slid aside already. Determined to speak with him, the lieutenant followed.

Outside, the sky was a deep and unbroken expanse of blue, mirrored in a hundred tiny pools. The exotic mix of shrubs and trees that grew among the ponds bent low under the press of the ocean breezes, only a few of them caught in the shadow of the soaring Academy building.

Though it was the height of summer, the air felt cool and moist on Kirk's face. It smelled of brine and something sugar-sweet that he had never taken the time to identify.

"Mitchell!" he called, shading his eyes.

The other man stopped and looked back at him, his hair lifting in the wind. He didn't say anything, but he seemed more than a little surprised.

The lieutenant caught up. "I want to talk to you."

"Is this round two?" Mitchell gibed, squinting in the glare of the bright Pacific sunlight.

Kirk shook his head. "Nothing like that. Just do me a favor and walk with me a minute. Okay?"

The other man shrugged. "I guess."

Together, they set out on one of the macadam paths that circumnavigated the pond-dappled garden. It took the lieutenant a moment to gather his thoughts, but Mitchell was patient.

"I owe you an apology," Kirk said at last.

Mitchell grunted. "I'll say."

"I mean it," the lieutenant told him. It came out a bit too earnestly.

"I know you do," said the other man. "That talent I have, remember?"

Mitchell was making it hard to forget. "It must have seemed pretty strange when I socked you," said Kirk.

"Well," the plebe replied, "I'll admit it wasn't exactly what I expected from a superior officer."

Again, the lieutenant wondered if the younger man was mocking him. But Mitchell was smiling at him, as if to assure his companion that his remark was meant good-naturedly.

"It wasn't what *I* expected, either," Kirk conceded. "But it happened almost every day of my first year at the Academy."

"Every day . . . ?"

The lieutenant winced at the memory. "I guess you haven't heard about me and Finnegan."

Mitchell shook his head. "Who was he?"

They passed within the shadow of the Academy building and the air grew chill. The breeze seemed to bite a little deeper there, too.

"My personal demon," Kirk explained. "An upper-classman who, for some reason I still can't fathom, just couldn't stand the sight of me. And he insisted on letting me know it at every opportunity."

His jaw clenched. How he had hated Finnegan.

"He used to sneak up on me when no one was looking," said the lieutenant, consciously trying to keep his hands from clenching into fists, "and beat the living daylights out of me. Mind you, I'm not just talking about a shot or two, though lord knows that would have been unreasonable enough. I mean a serious pounding."

Mitchell looked at him. "Why didn't you say something?"

Kirk grunted. "Go running to the commandant? I don't think so."

"The man deserved to be disciplined," the plebe argued.

"Maybe so," the lieutenant conceded. "But where I come from, we didn't go running to our moms and dads. We fought our own battles. So that's what I did—I fought back as best I could. Unfortunately, Finnegan was a much better scrapper than I was, so I always got the worst of it."

They passed the edge of the shadow and emerged into the sun again. It felt good on Kirk's skin.

"Interesting," said Mitchell.

"What is?"

"A guy who would squeal on his friend and protect his enemy."

The lieutenant felt a gout of anger rise inside him. "Finney's carelessness could have killed everyone on that ship," he said tightly. "I didn't want it to happen again on some other vessel." He glanced at the plebe. "Besides, I thought you approved of the way I handled that."

"I do," Mitchell told him. "In fact, I approve of the way you handled both those guys. I don't know too many people who would have done what you did in either case."

"If you're trying to suck up to your instructor . . ."

The underclassman shook his head. "Not my style."

Kirk believed him. "Anyway," he said, "when you came up behind me in the corridor, all I could think of was Finnegan sneaking up on me with a maniacal grin on his face. I just . . . reacted."

"Irrationally," Mitchell suggested.

The lieutenant yielded the point. "Irrationally."

"Actually," said the younger man, "a little irrationality's not a bad thing. If you can make it work for you, that is."

Kirk chuckled at the notion. "Really."

Despite his earlier assessment of Mitchell, the guy was actually beginning to grow on him. If they weren't so different, the lieutenant could almost have seen them becoming friends someday.

"Hey," said Mitchell, tilting his head appraisingly, "you don't happen to play racquetball, by any chance?"

"Are you kidding?" Kirk replied. "Racquetball's my middle name. I went to the county finals in Sioux City a couple of years ago."

"Pretty impressive," the underclassman told him. "Since you're such an expert, maybe I can convince you to give me a few pointers . . . say, this evening, after classes?"

The lieutenant was excited by the notion. "I'd be glad to," he told the younger man. "That is, if it won't interfere with your studies."

"My studies?" Mitchell echoed. He didn't give the lieutenant an answer. He just laughed.

Cadet Gary Mitchell let his superior officer lead the way onto the brightly lit, red and white racquetball court.

"Remember," said the plebe, watching the door in the back wall slide closed behind them, "you promised to take it easy on me."

Kirk glanced back at him over his shoulder. "I did?"

"Well, if you didn't," Mitchell said in a plaintive tone, "you should have. You went to the county finals, remember? In New York, there were no county finals. Hell, I'm not even sure we had a county."

The lieutenant chuckled at the remark. "You know, I almost believe you, Mitchell. But not quite."

"Call me Mitch," said the cadet. "On the court, at least. That's what people call me back home."

Kirk eyed him warily. "Mitch, then. But only when we're on the court."

"And what do I call you?" Mitchell asked.

The other man shrugged. "I guess Jim'll do. Anyway, that's what people called *me* back home."

The underclassman shook his head in mock amazement. "Those zany Iowans. You never know what they'll do next."

Taking the comment in the spirit it was intended, the lieutenant bounced his blue rubber ball and gave it a whack. It bounced off the front wall of the court and came back.

"Incidentally," Kirk observed, "I noticed you paid better attention in class today."

"Is that so?" asked Mitchell, returning his shot.

"It's absolutely so," said Kirk, whacking the ball back.

"Permission to speak freely?" asked the plebe.

"Permission granted," the lieutenant told him.

"If I paid better attention today," Mitchell said honestly, "it's because your lecture was a touch more interesting."

Kirk looked at him. "Do me a favor, all right?"

"What would that be?"

"Remind me not to give you permission to speak freely anymore."

Mitchell laughed. "I'll try to remember."

"Ready for a game?" asked the lieutenant.

"As ready as I'll ever be."

Kirk flipped Mitchell the ball. "Serve."

With a smile, Mitchell flipped it back. "You. I insist."

Smiling, the lieutenant took up a positon at the service line, about halfway between the front wall and the back one. Bending his knees and back, Kirk brought his racquet back with his right hand and bounced the ball low in front of him with his left.

Mitchell watched his opponent carefully, sizing him up. *Let's see,* he thought. *If this guy's as serious on the court as he is everywhere else, he'll be a cut-and-slash kind of player—the kind who puts everything he's got into each and every shot.*

As it turned out, the assessment was right.

Kirk's serve was a wicked blur of a line drive. It started out about six inches high, banged off the front wall and dropped as it neared the back wall. Worse, the serve was to Mitchell's left. He was forced to address it with his backhand, which wasn't half as good as his forehand.

No sooner had the ball hit the front wall again than Kirk pounced on it, plunking it into the crease where wall met floor. It didn't bounce out of there, either. It rolled out, giving Mitchell no chance at all to keep the volley going.

Score one for the upperclassman, he thought. But now that his theory about Kirk had been confirmed, it would be a different game. After all, Mitchell knew how to play the cut-and-slash type.

When Kirk served again, the plebe didn't try to slam the ball as his opponent had. He merely redirected it, using the force of Kirk's shot to bounce the ball off the ceiling.

The ball angled off the front wall, hit the floor, and bounded high in the air—so high, in fact, that Kirk had no choice but to try to race it to its ultimate destination. And that, Mitchell knew, was the rear, left-hand corner of the court.

To Kirk's credit, he beat the ball to its destination. But when he got there, he found he didn't have room to take a proper swing. As a result, the ball dropped and died, leaving the upperclassman nothing but perspiration for his trouble.

Mitchell retrieved the ball. "Lucky shot," he said, balancing it on the face of his racquet. "It won't happen again in a million years."

Kirk looked skeptical, but he didn't say anything. He just retreated to the backcourt and crouched in readiness.

As Mitchell stepped up to the service line, he cast a glance back at Kirk. The upperclassman was twirling his racquet in his hand, eagerly awaiting his adversary's serve.

This'll be easy, Mitchell thought. No doubt, Kirk was expecting the kind of beamlike serve he himself had launched. But Mitchell was going to give him something else entirely.

Because this game, like so many others, wasn't about how much sweat you put into it. It was about making adjustments. It was about going where your instincts led you. And at that moment, Mitchell's instincts were telling him to lob his serve into the corner—the same one that had been so good to him a few moments earlier.

He did just that. His ball hit high on the front wall and sailed back into the left-hand corner. What's more, it stayed out of Kirk's reach until the very last fraction of a second.

And then it dropped like a stone.

Perfect, Mitchell thought.

Unfortunately for him, Kirk had made an adjustment, too. Instead of charging into the corner, he stopped just short of it and waited for the ball to come down. Then, with a quick, economical flick of his racquet, Kirk sent the ball skimming back along the side wall.

The ball hit high on the front wall and came back to the same spot Mitchell had selected for it. Except this time, it was his turn to dig it out. Kirk's return having caught him by surprise, the younger man didn't move fast enough. The ball fell into the corner and didn't come out again.

Mitchell shook his head. He had been outfoxed. He didn't much like being outfoxed.

"Lucky shot," said Kirk.

The underclassman grunted. "Just serve."

It went on like that for some time, Mitchell's lobs against Kirk's rockets. Then the lieutenant began to diversify his game and the plebe responded in kind. Before Mitchell knew it, it was he who was hitting line drives and Kirk who was serving up lobs.

But no matter what tactics they adopted, no matter what tricks they pulled, they came out evenly matched. After an entire hour, they hadn't finished a single game.

"Had enough?" asked Kirk, his standard-issue gray T-shirt thoroughly soaked with sweat.

Mitchell grinned through his fatigue. "Funny, I was just going to ask you the same question."

"Good thing I'm taking it easy on you," said the upperclassman.

"You did go to the county finals," his opponent reminded him.

"Nobody in the county played the way you do."

"That's okay," said Mitchell, wiping perspiration from his brow with the back of his hand. "Nobody in the city played the way I do, either."

A moment later, realization dawned in Kirk's face. "Gary Mitchell, for crying out loud. Of course." He hit his forehead with the heel of his hand. "How could I be so dumb?"

"If you're determined to feed me straight lines," the younger man replied, "I'm eventually going to have to take advantage of them."

"You won the New York State singles championship last year."

Mitchell shook his head ruefully. "Lost it, actually. But—" He held up his hand, his thumb and forefinger spaced less than half an inch apart. "—I came this close."

Kirk smiled ruefully. "I should've known."

Suddenly, Mitchell heard a tapping on the back wall, which had a transparent window built into it. A woman's face was peering in at them.

She was an attractive woman, too—a Mediterranean type, with long, dark hair bound up in a sizable braid. She was making a T shape with her hands, signifying a time-out.

The cadet moved to the door in the wall. It slid

aside at his approach, revealing not one woman, but two. Both human, both cadets, both tall, slender, and good-looking. And their appearances were accentuated by the skimpiness of their racquetball gear.

"What can I do for you?" the plebe asked pleasantly.

"Time's up," said the Mediterranean type.

Mitchell was disappointed to hear it. He had really been enjoying himself. "Fair's fair," he responded nonetheless. "And," he added on an impulse, "you ladies are as fair as they come."

The women smiled and looked at one another. "Well," said the second one, a fiery, freckled redhead, "aren't you the flatterer."

"It's only flattery if it's not true," the cadet pointed out. "And in your cases, I'd say it's eminently true."

The darker woman grinned. "You've certainly made my day. But I have to tell you . . . we still want the court."

Mitchell nodded gallantly. "And you shall have it." Without looking at Kirk, he waved for the lieutenant to come along. "Come on, Jim. We know when we're not wanted."

"Say," said the redhead, stopping the underclassman in his tracks. She turned to her friend. "I have a better idea. Why don't we challenge these guys to a game of doubles? The losers can buy dinner."

The Mediterranean type thought about it for a moment, then nodded. "Could be fun, I suppose." She glanced at Mitchell, a playful look in her eyes. "That is, if they're not too tired from all their running around."

Mitchell smiled. He hadn't heard a better invitation since he arrived at the Academy. "I believe I can dredge up the strength for a game or two. Can't you, Jim?"

He turned to Kirk hopefully. But the lieutenant's expression had changed. It took Mitchell a moment to realize the man was blushing.

"Jim?" the cadet repeated.

Kirk cleared his throat. "I think I'd better call it a day."

Mitchell was aghast. The guy had to be kidding, right? He had to be pulling his friend's leg.

"Come on, now," the plebe said. "We've been challenged, Jim. You wouldn't want to turn down a challenge, would you?"

The lieutenant swallowed. "I've got to go," he said. Nodding stiffly to the women, he walked by them and left the court.

A crazy man, thought Mitchell, stunned by what he had seen. *I've decided to befriend a crazy man.*

"Oh, well," said the redhead, an undercurrent of genuine disappointment in her voice.

"I'll take a rain check," Mitchell told her. "A definite rain check. We'll do it another time, I promise." Then he took off after Kirk.

He found the upperclassman in the nearby locker room, where he had begun to strip off his sweat-darkened athletic shirt. Kirk glanced at him, but didn't say anything.

Seeing that they were alone in the room, Mitchell approached him. "With all due respect, Lieutenant . . . are you out of your corn-picking mind? Those

92

two women were clearly interested in getting to know us better, and you . . . you walked right out on them!"

The other man shrugged and pulled his locker open. "I just didn't think it was appropriate."

"To play racquetball with them?" asked Mitchell, bewildered.

Kirk nodded as he pulled out a towel. "They're cadets."

"You played racquetball with me," the plebe reminded him.

"That's different," Kirk told him.

"How is it different?" the underclassman pressed.

The lieutenant shot him a tortured look. "I believe you know how."

But this time, Kirk's emotions were too muddled for Mitchell to get an accurate reading on him. So he just took a stab at it. "You don't feel comfortable around women?"

The lieutenant shook his head. "I feel very comfortable around them. I even had a steady girlfriend for a while back home. But . . . I don't know. Women don't seem to feel comfortable around *me.*"

Mitchell tried to think about it calmly for a moment. "Well," he said, "I guess we shouldn't be all that surprised. With all those solemn looks and officious frowns of yours, you come off like a walking freezer unit."

Kirk looked at him. "Freezer unit?"

"That's what I said," the underclassman told him, standing his ground. "If a woman sat next to you, she'd probably get frostbite."

The lieutenant bit his lip. "Maybe you're right. Maybe I am a little . . . I don't know. Too serious."

"Damned right you are," Mitchell replied.

Kirk slung his towel around his neck and sat down on a bench near his locker. "But there's . . ." He shrugged.

"There's what?"

"There's a reason I act that way," the lieutenant said.

"I'm dying to hear it," the plebe responded.

"It's a long story," Kirk warned him.

"No problem. I've got nowhere to go," said Mitchell, "and a whole lot of time to get there."

The lieutenant took a deep breath. "All right, then. You asked for it. You see, back in high school, I was like anybody else—a regular guy, a slightly above average student. Certainly not Academy material."

That didn't sound right. "You? Not Academy material?"

"Believe it or not."

"But you're the A student to end all A students," Mitchell reminded him. "People talk about your grades with reverence in their voices."

"My grades here at the Academy have been great," the upperclassman conceded. "But they weren't that way then."

"Okay," said the plebe, willing to accept the information for the time being. "So what changed?"

Kirk sighed. "A couple of important people went out of their way to get me into this place. They put their reputations on the line, you could say, and I promised I wouldn't let them down."

"Important people."

"That's right," the lieutenant confirmed.

Mitchell started to ask who those people might be. Then he stopped himself. If Kirk had wanted to identify them, he would have.

"So," he said, "if I understand you correctly, you're getting top grades because you're afraid not to?"

The lieutenant mulled the analysis over for a second or two. "Those are your words," he decided, "not mine."

"But they're true, aren't they?"

Kirk shrugged. "In a manner of speaking, maybe."

The underclassman shook his head. "That's a hell of a motivation, if you ask me."

The lieutenant shrugged again. "I suppose."

Mitchell regarded Kirk as he sat there. Hunched over, his towel draped over his shoulders, the lieutenant looked pitiful despite all he had going for him. Pitiful and lost.

Every time he talked to the man, Mitchell found himself with a bigger job on his hands, a bigger challenge. But he wasn't a shirker. He'd undertaken Kirk's reclamation and he wasn't about to give up on the project now.

He just had to focus on one problem at a time. He chose to focus on the one nearest and dearest to him.

In other words, women.

"You know what, Kirk?" the underclassman declared. "You're a good guy underneath those lieutenant's bands. You're the kind of guy any girl would be glad to go out with, once she got past the freezer burns and saw what you were like." He stroked his chin thoughtfully. "The problem is convincing someone to give you a chance."

Kirk looked at him. "What do you mean?"

"Leave that to me," said Mitchell.

The lieutenant's expression became a stricken one. "You're not talking about a blind date, are you? Because you can forget it—I'm not going on any blind dates."

The plebe frowned. "I can't help you," he pointed out, "unless you let me."

"Then don't help," Kirk told him, waving away even the suggestion.

"You're sure?" Mitchell asked. "I mean, it could change your whole life."

"I'm sure," the upperclassman insisted.

Mitchell saw that Kirk was serious about it. But then, so was he.

The underclassman shrugged. "Suit yourself," he said. But in the privacy of his mind, he was already trying to think of a likely suspect he could steer in Kirk's direction.

Chapter Eight

As Mitchell took his seat in Kirk's Federation History class along with all the other cadets, he noticed the lieutenant standing in the front of the room, considering some notes on a computer padd.

A few moments later, the instructor looked up, the epitome of authority. It was difficult for Mitchell to reconcile this Kirk with the one who had stalked red-faced off the racquetball court.

"Does anyone have any questions about the Battle of Cheron?" the lieutenant asked abruptly. "About the tactics Earth forces employed or the reasons they employed them?"

No one did, apparently.

"Good," Kirk responded. "Then I'll proceed to our next topic—the aftermath of the battle. As you've learned, Earth forces won a decisive victory at Cheron. If we had wanted to, we could have pushed the Romulans all the way back to their homeworlds. But we declined to do that."

He looked straight at Mitchell.

"Any idea why, Cadet?"

Mitchell was surprised, to say the least. He thought he and the lieutenant had made their peace about his behavior in class. After all, he had paid attention the day before—or, at least, done a damned good job making it seem that way.

Now the man was sticking him with the very first question of the day. It didn't seem to the cadet like a coincidence.

Still, he had to come up with an answer of some kind. Putting his resentment aside, he turned the question over in his mind. And, of course, he studied Kirk's face for clues.

"Why didn't we push the Romulans all the way to their homeworlds . . ."

The lieutenant nodded. "That's what I asked, Mr. Mitchell."

Then, before the plebe could glean anything from him, Kirk turned away and took what seemed like a renewed interest in the padd he had left on his desk. All Mitchell could see of the lieutenant was the man's back.

It wasn't any accident, either. The underclassman knew that as surely as he knew his name. Kirk was trying to get him to answer the question without resorting to his intuition.

It left Mitchell with only one tool: common sense.

He applied it as best he could, under the circumstances.

"There wasn't anything to be gained by it," he responded.

Kirk didn't look at him. Instead, he continued to gaze at his padd. "Nothing at all, Cadet? Not even the destruction of the enemy's vastly productive shipbuilding facilities?"

Mitchell hadn't considered that aspect of it. "I suppose that might have been a worthwhile objective. But the Romulans could always have constructed new shipbuilding facilities."

"True," Kirk conceded, still intent on his padd. "But we could have destroyed the machinery that created new shipbuilding facilities. And yet, we didn't . . . why is that?"

The cadet felt the muscles in his jaw start to flutter. "Because it would have been too costly in terms of human lives."

"We had lost plenty of human lives to that point," the lieutenant noted grimly. "Why not expend a few more to make certain the Romulans could never trouble us again?"

Mitchell took a breath, let it out. He wasn't going to let Kirk get to him. He wasn't. "The Romulan worlds were too far away?"

"No," said the lieutenant, continuing to study his padd. "Remember, our propulsion systems were superior to theirs, and they had made it all the way to Earth. So why didn't we chase the Romulans to their lair the way they chased us?"

The cadet racked his brain, but he couldn't think of

any other possibilities. Finally, with a faintly mocking tone he hadn't intended, he replied, "I don't know, sir."

Kirk turned to him. "Don't know?" he echoed.

Mitchell felt the scrutiny of the other cadets. He didn't appreciate being embarrassed this way, especially when he didn't think he deserved it.

"That's correct," he replied.

"I see," said the lieutenant. He turned to another of his students, a slender woman with long, black hair whom Mitchell found rather attractive. "Cadet Ishida . . . why did we decide not to attack the Romulan homeworlds?"

"Because we didn't know if we could take them," Ishida answered. "We humans dug in when they came after Earth; more than likely, the Romulans would have defended their homeworlds with the same fervor."

Kirk nodded approvingly. "That's one reason—the uncertainty of accomplishing the objective. Can you think of another . . . Mr. Hagen?"

Hagen was a burly blond fellow. "Even if we managed to seize their homeworlds, sir, we could never have held them. The Romulans would eventually have made it too difficult for us."

"Good point," the lieutenant remarked. "Scientifically underdeveloped populations can be held in check for long periods of time—just ask the Klingons—but not a people as advanced in technology as the Romulans." He paused. "On the other hand, Mr. Hagen, we wouldn't have had to occupy the Romulans to destroy their warmaking capabilities. Isn't that true . . . Ms. Hilton?"

Hilton, a sturdy-looking woman with short, brown hair, responded crisply. "It is, sir. According to Torriente, the reason we didn't invade Romulus and Remus is we didn't want to make it personal."

"Personal . . . in what way?" asked the lieutenant.

Yes, Mitchell thought. *Tell us, Ms. Hilton.*

"The Romulans were a proud people, sir," the woman noted. "That much was obvious to us. If we handed them a humiliating defeat, they would have remembered. They would have held it against us. And as soon as they recovered, they would have come after us even harder."

"Can you give me an example of that?"

Hilton bit her lip. "Germany," she said after a moment, "after Earth's World War One. The Germans were so shamed by their defeat, they spent the next twenty years plotting their revenge."

Kirk smiled. "A little melodramatic, but essentially correct. Humble an enemy and all you may have done is postpone hostilities till he rearms himself. But if you're gracious enough to leave him with his self-respect . . . who knows? You may never have to fight him again."

A cadet named Ibrahim raised his hand.

The lieutenant recognized him. "Yes, Cadet?"

"Couldn't that strategy have backfired?" asked Ibrahim. "Couldn't the Romulans have seen our restraint as a sign of weakness?"

"They could have," Kirk allowed. "But it wasn't all

that likely, given what we had learned about them. After all, the Romulans themselves had exercised restraint on several occasions where further aggression wouldn't have gained them anything."

"But what if it hadn't been the Romulans?" Ibrahim ventured. "What if we were at war with a species so belligerent, so intractable, the only way to ensure our survival was to annihilate them . . . not only their warmaking capabilities, but the species itself?"

Kirk's expression became a sober one. "The annihilation of a living, thriving civilization is not an option—at least, not in my opinion. There's always another way, Mr. Ibrahim. You just have to find it."

The cadets absorbed that. Mitchell absorbed it, too.

But it wasn't the discussion at hand that really captivated him. It was the discussion he planned to have with Kirk after class.

When his class ended, Kirk watched the majority of his students file out of the room. But Mitchell remained in his seat, silent and unmoving, his expression one of marked belligerence.

The lieutenant couldn't say he was surprised. He had expected the underclassman to be a little taken aback by his behavior. In fact, he had been counting on it.

"Permission to speak freely," Mitchell said.

"I told you," Kirk replied, "I wouldn't give you that permission anymore." He paused. "But in this case, I'll make an exception."

"Thanks. Then, if it's not too much trouble, maybe you can tell me why you singled me out for ridicule."

"I didn't," said Kirk. "I asked you a question, the same way I asked questions of Ishida, Hagen, and Hilton. The difference is they gave me answers and you gave me a funny look."

"You turned your back on me."

"Damned right I turned my back on you," Kirk told him. "You're not in this class to make clever guesses, using talents other people don't have and can't take advantage of. You're here to learn."

Mitchell remained silent for a while. Finally, he said, "Be honest with me. Does this have anything to do with what happened yesterday on the racquetball court? Is it possible you're putting some distance between us so you won't have to be embarrassed that way a second time?"

Kirk shook his head. "It is has nothing to do with my behavior . . . and everything to do with yours."

"You're lying," said the cadet.

The lieutenant smiled, having already considered the charge in the confines of his own mind. "No. I'm telling you the truth. I guess even that intution of yours can be wrong once in a while."

Mitchell's eyes narrowed. "Just why is it so important to you that I toe the line? I mean, what difference does it make to *you* if I get by with my so-called clever guesses?"

Kirk looked at him. "Remember Ben Finney?"

The underclassman's brow creased. "What about him?"

"He was endangering the lives of his fellow crewmen. And if someone doesn't take you to task now, that's what you'll be doing someday. You'll find

103

yourself in a situation where you don't know what to do—"

"Because I didn't do my homework in Jim Kirk's Federation History class?" Mitchell's reaction was more instinct than argument, more counterpunch than coherent response.

"Maybe not," the lieutenant said evenly. "But I'll bet this isn't the only class you haven't been studying for."

It was true. He could see it in the underclassman's reaction. Mitchell had been coasting in his classes, just as he had coasted all his life, depending on his so-called flashes of insight to get him by. But he hadn't thought about it hurting anyone down the line. He hadn't thought about it in terms of Finney.

Now, thanks to Kirk's remark, he wouldn't be able to stop thinking that way. And the more he thought about it, the less he would like it . . . the less he would like himself.

At least, that was the lieutenant's plan.

"Tell you what," Kirk added for good measure. "I dare you to study. I dare you to do well in your classes without using your intuition. You like a challenge, don't you? Well, I'm throwing down the gauntlet. Let's see if you've got the guts to pick it up."

Mitchell regarded him for a long time. So long, in fact, that the lieutenant wondered if he had gone too far.

"You know," the plebe said at last, "it's been a while since I did something I didn't want to do. But it's also been a while since anyone suggested there was something I couldn't do."

Kirk smiled. "Then you'll accept my challenge?"

Mitchell nodded slowly. "Sure. Why not?"

"Good." The lieutenant cleared his throat. "And maybe next time, I won't run off the court at the first sign of the opposite sex."

The underclassman seemed surprised. "You mean you've reconsidered my offer to set you up with someone?"

Kirk grunted. "Let's not push it, all right?"

When Mitchell returned to his quarters, he found Brandhorst hunched over his workstation. *No surprise there,* he thought.

"Message for you," said the redhead.

Mitchell looked at his screen. Sure enough, the Starfleet icon in the upper right-hand corner was blinking red. Sitting down in front of the monitor, he brought up his communications menu.

There was only one message. It was from the Academy commandant, Admiral Pearson Everett.

Mitchell had a sudden, heartfelt premonition that he was getting jettisoned from the place for his study habits. Or, worse yet, for engaging in a slugfest with a certain lieutenant in a certain corridor.

No, he told himself. *That can't be right.*

He had been at the Academy less than a month for godsakes. No one except Kirk and Brandhorst knew how little he studied . . . and as far as he knew, no one had witnessed his fight with the lieutenant. The commandant must have been contacting him about something else.

His curiosity piqued, Mitchell called up the message. As he read it, he had the distinct feeling it was meant for someone else.

"What is it?" asked Brandhorst. He had looked up from his work, obviously more than a little curious himself. "Fan mail?"

Mitchell sat back in his chair and chuckled to himself. "No. Actually, it's an invitation."

His roommate swiveled in his chair to face him. "Really?"

"Uh-huh. To report to the *Republic,* where I'll be serving under a Captain Bannock. I'm to head over to the Academy transporter room at 0800 hours." He looked at Brandhorst. "This is a joke, right?"

The redhead was aghast. "Wait a minute. You're shipping out on the *Republic?* You, the guy who never even sits down at his workstation . . . except to research the schedule for the women's hypergravitational aerobics classes? And me—the hardest-working cadet in the entire freshman class—I get to stay home?"

Mitchell shrugged. "I feel your pain, Karl-Willem. Believe me, I can't figure it out either."

Brandhorst looked at him. "Unless . . ."

Suddenly, Mitchell had the same idea. "Kirk?"

"It's the only possible explanation."

Mitchell turned to the monitor again and smiled. "The man works in mysterious ways," he muttered.

"What'd you say?" asked Brandhorst.

Mitchell shook his head. "Nothing. Nothing at all."

Chapter Nine

KIRK WAS already standing on the circular transporter
pad with three other cadets when Mitchell walked
into the room.

"Cutting it a little close?" he asked the underclassman.

Unperturbed, Mitchell shrugged. "I prefer to think
of it as split-second timing, sir."

The transporter operator, who was standing behind
his control console, consulted his readouts. "Fifty-five
seconds to beam-up," he announced.

"You see?" said Mitchell, taking his place beside
Kirk on the platform. "I could've taken some time to
feed the plants."

"You don't have any plants," the lieutenant pointed
out.

"Details," the cadet replied. Then, under his breath, he said, "Tell me about this Captain Bannock."

Kirk smiled as he considered the subject. "He's one of my heroes."

"No, really," said Mitchell.

"I'm serious," the lieutenant assured him. "Eight years ago, when Rollin Bannock was captain of the *Excalibur,* he devised and led the flanking maneuver that cost the Klingons the Battle of Donatu Five."

"I'm impressed," said the plebe.

"Really?" the lieutenant asked warily.

"Well . . . no."

"You should be," Kirk told him.

"And why's that?"

"Bannock's strategy at Donatu Five," said the upperclassman, "is considered one of the most brilliant gambits in modern military history. And in case you're interested, Bannock was also responsible for convincing the Axanarri to sign a treaty with the Federation last year, earning himself and several members of his crew the Palm Leaf of Axanar."

Mitchell glanced at him knowingly. "Several members . . . including a certain Lieutenant Kirk, I'll bet."

"That would be a good bet," said the lieutenant. "But what I got had nothing to do with it. I just admired the way Bannock handled the Axanarri. I hope I'm half the negotiator he is when I get my chance at command."

"Ready to transport," said the operator.

"Ready," Kirk responded, as the ranking officer.

"Energizing," the operator reported.

"So if this Bannock's been carting cadets around," said Mitchell, "he's probably something of a father figure . . . yes?"

The lieutenant sighed, recalling Bannock's demeanor. "You've got a lot to learn, Cadet."

Suddenly, they were no longer in the Academy's spacious transporter facility. They were standing on an identical platform in the considerably smaller transporter room of a starship.

In addition to the vessel's transporter operator, there were two officers standing in front of them. One was a powerful-looking, olive-skinned fellow in the red shirt and gold bands of a security chief. The other was a wiry man with a deeply lined face and a shock of thick, gray hair, whose heavy-browed stare could have cut duranium.

"Lieutenant Kirk," said the older man, who happened to be wearing the gold shirt of command. "Good to see you again."

Kirk allowed himself a smile. "Good to see you, Captain Bannock. And you as well, Commander Rodianos."

The security officer inclined his head. "Welcome back."

The captain's eyes, which were an ice-pale shade of blue, slid in the direction of the other cadets. "Brought me another batch of cannon fodder, have you, Kirk?"

"Aye, sir," said the lieutenant, accustomed to Bannock's bone-dry sense of humor. "I've already notified their next of kin."

The captain harrumphed, poker-faced. "As long as I'm in charge, I'll make the jokes around here, Mr. Kirk."

The lieutenant nodded. "Duly noted, sir," he responded.

Bannock scanned the faces of the underclassmen on the transporter platform. "I'm Captain Bannock," he told them. "This fellow here," he said, tilting his head in the security officer's direction, "is Lieutenant Commander Rodianos, my security chief. He's the one you'll have to answer to when you're not where you're supposed to be. Understood?"

"Yes, sir," the cadets answered with one voice.

The captain nodded approvingly. "You make a nice chorus. Now, there are a lot more of you slated to beam up, so if I were you I'd get the hell off that transporter pad."

Immediately, the cadets got down from the platform. Naturally, Kirk noted, Mitchell was the last to respond to Bannock's suggestion. The captain appeared to notice as well, though he seemed disinclined to comment on it.

"I've scheduled a briefing in the lounge," he continued. "Deck three in half an hour. Any questions at this time?"

There weren't any.

"Good," said Bannock. "I like a group that knows how to listen." Then he hooked a thumb over his shoulder. "So what are you waiting for? Get the blazes out of here."

Kirk led the way out of the transporter room into the corridor beyond. As Mitchell caught up with him, the underclassman made a face. "The man sure knows how to roll out the welcome mat."

"Consider yourself lucky," the lieutenant told him. "You caught the captain in a good mood."

While Mitchell was contemplating what Bannock's bad moods were like, Kirk showed the cadets to their quarters.

Mitchell did his best to keep up with Kirk, who negotiated the curving corridors of the *Republic* with practiced ease.

The plebe had never been out in space before, much less on a starship, much less on a starship of this size. The Constitution-class vessel seemed to sprawl in every direction, presenting him with one splendid, silver-blue passageway after another.

Fortunately, the *Republic* boasted state-of-the-art turbolifts, capable of transporting a person from any location in the ship to any other location—and all in no more than a few seconds. All one had to do was punch in one's destination and the lift did the rest.

Thanks to the turbolifts, even a newcomer could get anywhere he wanted. Which was why Kirk's insistence on guiding him through the ship seemed a little unnecessary.

"You know," Mitchell said, "I probably could have made it to the briefing on my own. You didn't have to give me a personal escort."

"Yes, I did," the lieutenant disagreed. "It's the only way I could make sure you'd get there on time."

"Since when did you become my keeper?" the underclassman wondered.

Kirk glanced at him. "About the same time you became mine."

Mitchell barely had a chance to ponder the remark when he spotted the entrance to the ship's lounge. As he followed his friend into the room, he saw that a couple dozen cadets were already seated around the tables inside. Some looked familiar, others only vaguely so.

But only one of them really held his interest—a blue-skinned Andorian with long legs, big black eyes, and hair like spun silver. Her antennae were delicate stalks protruding from the center of her head.

"My, my," Mitchell muttered appreciatively.

Then he glanced at Kirk and saw that the lieutenant had noticed the Andorian as well. But where Mitchell had taken the sight in stride, Kirk was standing there with his mouth half-open.

"Easy, champ," said Mitchell, low enough so no one else could hear him. "Just breathe, okay?"

"Okay," Kirk muttered.

"Good," said the plebe. "Don't stop."

Then he took the lieutenant's arm and ushered him into the room. Choosing a table as far from the Andorian as possible, he sat down and pulled Kirk by his sleeve into the chair beside him.

Fortunately, no one noticed the lieutenant's dumbfoundedness, because the *Republic*'s command staff chose that moment to make its entrance. As the officers took their places at the far end of the room, Mitchell saw Bannock among them.

Rodianos was conspicuous by his absence. But

then, Mitchell mused, it was against regulations to leave the bridge unoccupied, even in Earth orbit. Even he knew that.

"Thanks a bunch for coming," the captain told the assembled cadets, his tone nothing short of sardonic. "For everyone's sake, I'll try to make this as brief as possible. You've all met me and Security Chief Rodianos, much to your chagrin. Now you'll meet the rest of my officers."

First, he introduced a friendly, almost matronly-looking woman with graying brown hair pulled back into a bun. Her name, he said, was Ellen Mangione; she had been his exec since he took command of the *Republic*.

"In this case," Bannock noted, "familiarity has bred only respect. See that you treat the commander with it as I do."

Next came a Vobilite named Miyko Tarsch, who served as ship's doctor. Tarsch had the mottled red skin and protruding jaw tusks common to males of his species, but his yellowing thicket of white scalp spines showed he was getting on in years.

Science officer Jord Gorfinkel was third in line. A lean fellow with aquiline features and curly brown hair, Gorfinkel nodded a bit awkwardly to the cadets when he was introduced.

The last to be identified was Hogan Brown, the *Republic*'s chief engineer. Brown was a black man with light green eyes and a full, dark beard. When he smiled, he showed all his teeth.

"The rest of the crew," the captain pointed out,

"has been granted shore leave on Earth. They'll be enjoying themselves in history-soaked cities and exotic climes while my command staff and I remain here to groom the future of the Fleet. In case you haven't figured it out yet, that's *you.*"

Their voyage, Bannock went on, would be "a simple one. We're to conduct a two-week sweep across the Federation side of the Klingon Neutral Zone, during which time you will assist in updating planetary surveys. Of course, by the end of our mission, we'll be skirting a sector claimed by neither the Klingons nor the Federation—but we have no plans to explore it. That's a job for a more experienced crew."

Mitchell glanced at his friend Kirk. The lieutenant had managed to close his mouth and turn his attention to the captain, but he couldn't help stealing a look at the Andorian from time to time.

"We've all had plenty of experience with training voyages," Bannock said, "so we know what kinds of behavior you promising young men and women are capable of. As a result, we'll be keeping a close eye on you."

Thoughtful of you, Mitchell mused.

"But," the captain added, "if you keep your noses clean and do your job, you'll beam off the *Republic* with a slew of experience and a new insight into your studies."

One of the cadets, a woman with long, blonde hair, raised her hand. Bannock recognized her.

"Will we get a chance to express our preferences as to which duties we'll perform?" she asked.

A ripple of laughter ran through the line of command officers. The captain's eyes crinkled at the corners, but he refrained from laughing along with his staff.

"We've got all that information in our files," he told the cadet. "If we've got any questions beyond that, we know where to find you."

Obviously, Mitchell mused, it wasn't the answer the cadet had been hoping for. Nonetheless, she would have to live with it.

"If there are no other questions," Bannock said dryly, "you can check a monitor for your duty assignments. They begin in a few minutes. Good morning and good luck."

As the captain and his staff took their leave of the cadets, Mitchell turned to Kirk. "Sounds exciting," he said, making no effort to hide the sarcasm in his voice.

"It's not," the lieutenant confirmed. Unable to help himself, he watched the Andorian cross the lounge. "But it's a necessary step if you're after a berth on a starship."

Mitchell smiled. "And what are you after?"

Kirk turned to him, caught off-balance. "What's that?"

"I asked what you were after, Lieutenant. But don't bother answering—I think I already know."

Kirk's brow creased. Then he glanced at the departing figure of the Andorian. "You mean her?" he asked.

"I mean her," said the plebe.

"She's just another cadet."

"Yeah, right," said Mitchell. "And the Romulan Wars were just another skirmish. You want that woman and you know it."

The lieutenant looked at the underclassman askance. "Don't get any ideas, all right?"

"What do you mean?" Mitchell inquired innocently.

"I told you before, I don't want you setting me up with anyone—least of all, her."

"Why not?" the plebe pressed.

"Because she's an alien," Kirk pointed out. "I've got enough problems with human women."

Man, Mitchell thought. *Has he got a lot to learn.*

"There's nothing to it," he told the lieutenant. "Aliens are no different from other women."

"How would you know?" Kirk asked.

How indeed, thought the cadet.

"Excuse me," he said, "but if you recall, we spent nearly a month at the Academy before this mission came through. I hope you don't think I was ignoring my work for nothing."

The upperclassman looked skeptical. "No . . ."

"Oh, yes. And I'm here to tell you there's no special trick to it. You open up to them and they'll open up to you, just like any human woman." He leaned closer to his friend. "So what do you say?"

Kirk shook his head emphatically from side to side. "I don't want any help. I mean it."

Mitchell grinned. "Not even a little?"

"I'm leaving now," said the lieutenant, "to see to my assignment. If you're smart, you'll do the same thing."

Mitchell sighed. "You'll be passing up the opportunity of a lifetime."

Kirk blushed. "Don't even think about it," he warned the cadet. Then he got up and started to leave the lounge.

"Hey!" said Mitchell.

The lieutenant stopped.

"Meet you in the gym after first shift, right? Oh-one-hundred hours," the underclassman suggested.

Kirk thought about it for a moment, as if trying to see what angle his friend might be playing this time. Finally, he nodded. Then he turned again and made his exit.

Mitchell shook his head in wonderment. *What a piece of work you are, James T. Kirk.*

Chapter Ten

KIRK GAZED at the monitor in his quarters and smiled.

He had called up the *Republic*'s duty schedule, only to see that he had been given the ship's helm—and not just on the part-time basis he had enjoyed the year before. This time, the post was all his.

Of course, he couldn't steer the ship all day and all night, nor did he want to. But it would be up to him as to who took over, for how long, and under what circumstances.

It was a lot of responsibility for a cadet, even one who had been given officer's bands. But Captain Bannock had a lot of faith in Kirk. The man had said as much to his face.

Suddenly, this mission seems a lot more exciting, the lieutenant mused. Rising from his workstation, he left his quarters and made his way out into the corridor, then headed for the nearest turbolift. The doors parted as he approached, revealing an empty compartment. He entered.

As the doors closed again, Kirk thought about Mitchell's offer. Contrary to what he had said in the lounge, the Andorian wasn't just another cadet to him. In point of fact, he found her extremely attractive.

If Mitchell could have been guaranteed that the attraction would be mutual, he might have let the cadet arrange a date for him. Hell, he might have begged him for it.

But the lieutenant knew himself too well. He was no longer the happy-go-lucky Jim Kirk he had been back in Iowa—and no woman would ever fall for a man who had become . . . what had Mitchell called him?

A walking freezer unit.

Maybe someday, Kirk mused, he would have the luxury of studying less and taking life as it came. Maybe someday, he would be able to focus on something besides his studies.

But every time he thought of Captain April or Admiral Mallory—good people who had put their reputations on the line to get him into Starfleet Academy—he felt compelled to show them they had made the right decision.

Kirk had barely completed his thought when the lift doors opened again, admitting him to the *Republic*'s bridge. Briskly, he circumvented the captain's chair, which was empty for the time being, and headed for the sleek curve of the helm-navigation console.

Chief Rodianos was sitting there at the moment, performing both functions. Clearly, the lieutenant thought, he would have to do the same.

"Mr. Kirk," said Rodianos, turning in his seat. He smiled. "Think you can handle her?"

The lieutenant smiled back at him. "I guess we'll see, sir."

"I guess we will," the security officer agreed good-naturedly. Getting up, he turned his console over to Kirk and made his way to the aft security station, no doubt to run some more system diagnostics.

Savoring the moment, the lieutenant sat down and took Rodianos's place at the helm. The controls and monitors there looked as familiar as if he had seen them only the day before, though it had been months since he last set foot on the *Republic*.

A quick scan of the console showed him that everything was in order. External sensors, both long-range and short-range, checked out fine. So did navigational deflectors, weapons arrays, and both sets of engines.

Kirk was about to check his course-deviation plotter when the image on his warp-drive monitor changed, drawing his attention. Somehow, the green-on-black graphic that should have described the rate of plasma release had given way to something else . . . something unexpected. . . .

A human face.

And not just any human face, the lieutenant realized. This one was familiar to him, though he wished at that moment it weren't. Worse, the face was grinning at him, leering at him, as if it had just heard the universe's best and biggest joke.

Kirk cursed beneath his breath, then peered back over his shoulder at Chief Rodianos. Fortunately, the brawny security officer hadn't looked up from his bridge station.

The lieutenant turned back to his monitor. The face was still there, still smirking like crazy. Come to think of it, Kirk mused, maybe crazy was the operative word here.

"Mitchell," he whispered between tightly clenched teeth.

"At your service," said the cadet. "I thought you might like some company up there."

Kirk leaned closer to the audio receiver in his control board. "Aren't you supposed to be doing something?"

"Probably," came the reply. "But could it be any more important than visiting with my friend, Jim Kirk? We're still meeting in the gym, right? Oh-one-hundred hours, as I recall?"

"Dammit, Mitchell . . . do you know what they'll do to you if they catch you hacking into the navigation controls?"

"Oh, I don't know . . . congratulate me on my initiative? Pin a medal on me, if they can find one in my size?"

Kirk's teeth ground together. "You're an idiot."

The cadet looked at him dubiously. "Are you qualified to make that kind of analysis, Lieutenant?"

It was no use. The man was incorrigible.

"Get out of there," he told Mitchell. "Now. That's an order."

Suddenly, Kirk had the uncomfortable feeling that there was someone directly behind him. Someone looking over his shoulder. He whirled in his seat—and found himself face-to-face with the steely-eyed visage of Captain Bannock.

"What's going on up there?" Mitchell asked, unable to see what the lieutenant was seeing. "Am I missing something good?"

The captain regarded Kirk for a moment, the lines around his mouth drawn into a deep, forbidding frown. Then he leaned past the younger man and addressed Mitchell's image on the monitor.

"I believe the lieutenant gave you an order," he told the plebe. "Let's see if you're more inclined to follow his directions than you are mine."

Kirk saw his friend blanche with surprise.

"Aye, sir," Mitchell replied. "I mean, I am, sir. Inclined to follow his orders, sir."

A moment later, the underclassman was gone, and the plasma-release graphic had been restored to the screen.

Bannock turned back to the lieutenant. "Whatever the problem with your monitor was," he said, "I believe I've fixed it for you."

Kirk didn't know what to say to that. Finally, he just nodded.

The captain harrumphed. "Don't mention it."

* * *

Less than five minutes after he had been discovered on his friend's monitor, Mitchell received a summons from Captain Bannock.

Damn, he thought. *What have I gotten myself into now?*

Leaving engineering, where he was supposed to have been running diagnostic routines instead of hacking into places where he didn't belong, the cadet made his way to the *Republic*'s briefing room. When he got there and the doors opened for him, he saw that the captain was already seated inside.

Bannock was studying the two-sided monitor in the center of the table. It displayed a personnel file. Mitchell didn't have to see the headshot that accompanied the text to know whose file it was.

"Sir," said the cadet, as the doors slid closed behind him.

The captain took a moment to finish his reading. Then he looked up, the glare of the monitor illuminating his craggy features. He didn't ask Mitchell to sit down.

Bad sign, thought the cadet. *Very bad sign.*

"Interesting file," said Bannock. "Back in New York, you were quite the resourceful young man."

"Thank you, sir."

"Yes," said the captain, drawing the word out. "Very resourceful. A real credit to the institutions you attended."

Mitchell nodded. "Thank you again, sir."

Bannock regarded him. "On the streets of New York, you must have been something, Cadet. You must have been the king of the hill. But you're not on the streets of New York anymore, are you?"

Here it comes, thought the plebe. "No, sir, I'm not."

"You're enrolled at Starfleet Academy now. And at the Academy, you can't get by on cleverness alone."

Mitchell nodded. "I'll remember that, sir."

The captain's eyes narrowed. Clearly, he was wondering if the younger man was saying that just to appease him.

Frowning, he said, "Tell me, Cadet. Where would you like to be ten years from now?"

Mitchell hadn't thought about it. "Ten years, sir?"

"That's right."

The underclassman considered the question. "On a starship," he replied at last, unable to think of any better answer.

"As what?" asked Bannock. "Captain? First officer?"

Mitchell shrugged. "As anything, sir. I just want to be part of it."

"Part of it?"

"The adventure, sir."

Bannock grunted. "The adventure," he said, as if he were describing something he had found on the sole of his boot. He shook his head. "That's just what I was afraid of."

Mitchell didn't understand. He said so. He also didn't like the tone of the captain's voice, but he kept that part to himself.

"Listen," Bannock told him. "There's nothing wrong with simply wanting to contribute. Not everyone has the tools to qualify for command. But others in the Academy *do* have the tools, and Jim Kirk is one of them."

Mitchell felt a surge of resentment. He swallowed it back.

"If I may say so," the captain went on, "a guy like you isn't going to be a positive influence in Jim Kirk's life. He's not going to be an asset with regard to Kirk's career prospects." He leaned forward, his eyes boring holes into the cadet's psyche. "Do I need to spell it out for you, Mr. Mitchell? Or can you read between the lines?"

Mitchell's jaw clenched. "I can read fine, sir," he answered in the steadiest voice he could manage.

"Good," said Bannock. "Then remember this conversation, because I don't wish to repeat it."

"Aye, sir."

"Goodbye, Mr. Mitchell. You're dis—"

"Permission to speak freely, sir," said the cadet.

The captain raised an eyebrow. "Permission granted—though I have a feeling you're determined to speak freely with or without my permission."

For a moment, Mitchell wondered if the man had some flashes of insight of his own. Then he dragged his mind back on course.

"I appreciate the advice with regard to Lieutenant Kirk," he said. "I think he's got a lot of potential myself. But I should tell you, Captain . . . I have no intention of keeping my distance from him, regardless of what you think of the situation."

The muscles in Bannock's temples rippled dangerously. "Is that so?" he grated, his eyes hard as rocks.

"Yes, it is. If you want to boot me out of the Academy," Mitchell continued, "I suppose that's your prerogative, and there isn't much I can do about it. But I'm not going to abandon a friendship just because some high-ranking muckety-muck tells me to."

The captain turned livid. "Is that all?"

"Yes," said the cadet. He straightened, sensing that things had become formal again. "That's all, sir."

Bannock regarded him with anger and contempt. "I wish I could order you to leave Kirk alone," he rasped. "Hell, I wish I could ship you back to New York with your tail tucked between your legs. Unfortunately, it's not that easy. But I'm going to do everything in my power to drive a wedge between you and Kirk. Is that understood, Cadet?"

"It is," Mitchell assured him.

The captain's eyes blazed with hellish fury. "It is . . . what?"

Feeling his cheeks burning like twin suns, the underclassman thrust his chin out. "It is, *sir.*"

Bannock let him stand there for a second or two, as a reminder of who was in charge. Then he said, in a low voice, "Dismissed."

Mitchell turned and walked out of the room, the door whispering open in front of him and then whispering shut again in his wake. It was only when he was out in the corridor by himself that he stopped, looked back, and muttered a long, elaborate curse.

Suddenly, he realized how he must have looked, swearing at the briefing-room door . . . and he started laughing at himself. *Kirk should see me now,* he thought. *He'd eat this up.*

That is, he mused, *just as soon as he got done chewing me out for that stunt I pulled. Unfortunately, I'm going to be hearing about that one for a long time to come.*

Still chuckling, Mitchell made his way back to engineering.

Chapter Eleven

BY THE TIME Kirk got to the *Republic*'s gymnasium, he was primed and ready for a fight.

It had been one thing for Mitchell to test the patience of a newly minted lieutenant. That, Kirk had been able to tolerate. But to demonstrate complete and utter contempt for the authority of someone like Captain Bannock?

That, he told himself, was another matter entirely.

No doubt, the captain had already taken Mitchell to task for it. But as far as the lieutenant was concerned, whatever Bannock had said wasn't enough. He, too, had a few choice words for his friend.

As an accessory to a violation of the rules, Kirk was lucky he hadn't been stripped of his rank on the spot. And if anything of that nature happened again, Bannock wouldn't be anywhere near that compassionate. The lieutenant had no illusions about that.

He watched the gym doors slide open in front of him and marched inside. But when Kirk entered the room, he found himself alone with the stainless-steel exercise equipment. Mitchell wasn't there yet.

Taking a deep breath, the lieutenant tried his best to put a lid on his frustration. The least the man could have done was get there on time. But, no . . . he had denied Kirk even that small satisfaction.

The upperclassman scrutinized the high bar in the center of the gym. *It makes no sense to stand around and wait,* he told himself. *I might as well use my time here to good advantage.*

Approaching the freestanding tray at the side of the apparatus, Kirk removed some chalk powder and rubbed it into his hands. Then he took a position beneath the bar, leaped, and gripped it.

As always, the lieutenant hung there for a second or two, feeling his muscles stretch, oxygenating his blood with slow, deep breaths. Then he began swinging back and forth.

This time, he wasn't going to try any seriously intricate maneuvers. Part of his mind was still dwelling on his pal Mitchell, and one didn't undertake a triple somersault when one's attention was divided. That was the surest path to a crippling injury, maybe even suicide.

Instead, Kirk decided, he would try a few simple stunts. Swinging as hard and as high as he could, he elevated himself to a handstand, then changed his grip so he was facing the other way. As he swung forward again, he did so with enough force to reach another handstand. Again, he shifted his grip on the bar and swung back in the opposite direction.

His arms tiring, the lieutenant opted for a demanding but ultimately rather simple dismount. Rolling forward into a position below the bar, he swung forward and back a few times to work up momentum. Then, on his third backswing, he extended his legs on either side and jerked himself forward over the bar, feeling like a missile shot from a catapult.

As it happened, Kirk didn't execute the move very well. His rear end barely cleared the bar as he sailed over it. And when he landed on the mat below, he was a little off-balance.

Still, it garnered him a polite round of applause from somewhere behind him. *So he's finally here,* the lieutenant thought. He turned to face Mitchell, still breathing heavily from his exertions, his anger with the cadet springing to the fore.

But it wasn't Gary Mitchell he found himself facing across a gym mat. It was the Andorian female he had seen earlier in the *Republic*'s lounge . . . the one with soft-looking skin and big black eyes and hair that looked like finely spun platinum.

Kirk tried to speak, to say something to her . . . but he couldn't. His mouth had suddenly gone dry as a desert. He managed to make his lips move, but nothing came out.

Of all the people he might have seen here, he thought. Of all the absolutely beautiful, compelling, captivating individuals who could have walked into the place . . .

Then it occurred to him that this was too perfect to be a coincidence. Someone had to have engineered it. Someone with a fierce desire to set him up with an attractive woman.

He gritted his teeth. *Mitchell.*

"Hello," said the Andorian. She came forward and held out a slender blue hand, her antennae bending subtly in the lieutenant's direction. "My name's Phelana. Phelana Yudrin."

It was too late for him to escape, as he had the other day on the racquetball court. Trapped, he shook the cadet's hand, discovering that her skin was every bit as soft as it looked.

"Kirk," he said, though it sounded to him as if he had uttered little more than a grunt.

"Kirk," she repeated. "Is that your first name?"

"No," he replied. "Jim."

Phelana smiled at him. "Kirk Jim? Or Jim Kirk?"

He tried to smile back. "Yup. I mean . . . Jim Kirk."

Her brow wrinkled. "Is everything all right?"

"Er . . . just fine," he managed.

It was a significant improvement. Maybe soon he would get out a *two*-syllable word.

"I hope you're not done," the Andorian remarked.

"Done?" Kirk repeated, at a loss.

"With your routine," Phelana told him. She indicated the high bar with a lift of her delicate chin. "It was a great routine. I mean, what little I saw of it."

He laughed—except it came out as a giggle. "Thanks," he said, though inside he was cursing himself.

"I'd like to see more of it," Phelana said. "That is, if you're not all worn out already."

Despite his tongue-tied responses, she didn't seem at all bored or uncomfortable with him. In fact, she seemed to like him.

"Nope," he answered. "Not worn out. Not at all."

She stepped back and folded her arms across her chest. Go ahead, she seemed to say. Impress me.

Kirk knew it would be more intelligent to rest for a moment. After all, he was still bushed from his last go-around with the bar, still doing his best to catch his breath.

But when a beautiful woman asked a man to show off for her, what choice did he really have in the matter?

Mitchell was sure Kirk was going to kill him. As if it weren't enough that he had roused the ire of Captain Bannock, he was also going to be late for their appointment in the gym.

Fortunately, he had an excuse this time. Just as the cadet was about to leave engineering, a grinning Chief Brown had insisted that he remodulate the ship's shield frequencies. There wasn't any reason for it that Mitchell could see, but he was hardly in a position to argue with the man.

All he could do was work as quickly as possible, get Brown to approve his work, and hightail it out of engineering. Now he found himself jogging along the corridor that led to his quarters, hoping to change and get down to the gym before too much more time went by.

But as he negotiated a bend in the passageway, he saw the brawny form of Chief Rodianos approaching from the other direction. Suddenly, he got the feeling that Rodianos was there looking for him.

That's got to be wrong, Mitchell told himself. *I just got done with my shift. What would Rodianos want with me?*

Just as he thought that, the security chief stopped in front of him. "Mr. Mitchell," he said. "Just the man I was looking for. I've got an assignment for you."

Suddenly, all the pieces came together. This was Bannock's doing, the cadet realized. Now that he thought about it, he wondered if the shield remodulations hadn't been Bannock's idea, too.

"Wouldn't it be easier to just throw me in the brig, sir?"

Rodianos looked at him. "The brig?"

"You know," said Mitchell, "for being Lieutenant Kirk's friend. That seems to be a punishable offense around here."

The big security chief shook his head. "I don't know what you're talking about, mister—and to tell you the truth, I don't want to know. Now, if it's all right with you, we're scheduled to meet a number of other cadets in the ship's lounge."

"At the captain's suggestion, no doubt."

Rodianos's eyes narrowed. "I'd be glad to discuss that with you, Cadet, if I thought it was even remotely any of your business."

Mitchell sighed. Obviously, Bannock was making good on his threat to keep Kirk and his friend apart. And for the moment, at least, there wasn't a whole lot he could do about it.

"Anything else?" asked the security chief.

Mitchell shook his head. "Nothing, sir."

Together, they made the trek to the *Republic*'s lounge.

As Kirk swung forward with all the centrifugal force he could muster, he thought his arms were going to tear out of their sockets. Truthfully, he should have quit thirty seconds earlier.

But he had felt his audience's admiration for him grow with every muscle-straining maneuver, and he couldn't have imagined a lovelier audience if he had tried. With that in mind, it was difficult to stop.

And now, he was going to attempt the triple flip again. If the lieutenant had had his wits about him, he might have acknowledged that he was too winded, too bone-tired to try anything so elaborate. But he hadn't had his wits about him since he turned and saw Phelana standing in the gym.

At the high point of his swing, he released his grip on the bar and brought his knees up, just as he had the other day at the Academy. As he counted, the gym rotated around him. One. Two . . .

Suddenly, Kirk had the feeling that he wasn't going to complete the third somersault. Grabbing his knees, he dug them into his chest as far as they would go and leaned back for all he was worth.

Even so, his feet didn't hit the floor flat. He landed

on his toes and stumbled forward, thrusting his hands out to keep him from falling on his face. As it was, he hit the mat with his shoulder, jamming it—and causing himself no small amount of pain.

But all in all, he could hardly complain. He had avoided breaking any bones, his neck prominent among them.

As he turned over, he was surprised to find himself looking up into the face of a blue-skinned, platinum-haired angel. Phelana was leaning over him on all fours, concern evident in her every delicate feature. Even her antennae seemed to quiver.

"Are you all right?" she asked.

The lieutenant nodded, though his shoulder hurt like the dickens. "Fine," he told her, unable to keep from noticing how good she smelled. But then, Andorian women were known for the allure of their pheromones.

Phelana extended her hand and he took it. Together, they lifted him off the gym mat. The woman still appeared worried, though.

"You're certain you're all right?"

He was going to repeat his earlier answer, then gave up the pretense. "Actually . . . I'm afraid I did something to my shoulder."

"Do you need to go to sickbay?"

Kirk rotated his arm in its socket. "I don't think so. Probably, all it needs is some rest."

"Good." The Andorian shrugged. "I would hate to think you'd hurt yourself on my account."

"It wouldn't have been your fault," he insisted. "I was going to try a few of those moves anyway."

Phelana looked at him askance.

"Then again," he conceded unexpectedly, "maybe not."

It occurred to the lieutenant that Mitchell had been right. The Andorian wasn't so different from Earth women after all. In fact, he felt right at home with her.

"That was very dashing of you," she noted. "Showing off for me, I mean. Very sweet."

Kirk would have done a lot more than that for her, had he been given the chance. In fact, he would have done anything. But he didn't think it would be a good idea to say so.

Phelana smiled at him, but not wholeheartedly. There was something holding her back, he realized, something he couldn't put his finger on.

Finally, she said, "I have a confession to make."

"A confession?" he echoed.

"Yes." Her antennae seemed to recoil. "You see, I'd heard about you from some of the second-year cadets. They said you were . . ."

"I was what?" the lieutenant prompted.

The Andorian frowned. "I believe the term was 'a know-it-all jerk.'"

It hit him like a blow to the stomach. "Really."

"Of course," she added quickly, "those were their words, not mine."

"I understand," he assured her.

Kirk was a lot more unsettled by the knowledge than he let on. *So that's what my fellow upperclassmen think of me—or some of them, at least. But then,* he told himself, *maybe I shouldn't be all that surprised.*

They had to be a little jealous of his success, a little

resentful about his meteoric promotion. It was only natural.

"Anyway," Phelana continued, her black eyes gleaming, "I don't think you're a jerk at all. In fact . . . I think you're rather nice."

The lieutenant felt himself blush. He had an urge to turn away from her, to excuse himself and retreat to the safety of his quarters. But he didn't. He stood there, blush and all.

"Thanks," he said. "And . . ."

Kirk found it hard to get the rest out, but the Andorian waited patiently for him to finish. Take all the time you want, she seemed to say, all the time you need.

". . . I think you're rather nice, too," he finished at last.

She rolled her eyes. "Yes. Nice and nervous."

Kirk looked at her. "You? I mean . . . about what?"

Phelana shrugged. "Everything, really. This is my first mission and . . . to tell you the truth, I'm afraid I'll embarrass myself."

He smiled, enchanted by her vulnerability. "I was nervous too, my first time out. But, really, there's nothing to be concerned about. We're here more to learn than to be . . ."

Suddenly, he became all too aware of how close they were standing.

". . . to be . . ."

Close enough for him to reach out and caress her cheek. Close enough for him to fold his arms around her waist and bury his face in her neck and revel in her scent.

". . . judged," he finished absently.

Part of the lieutenant wanted to withdraw, dreading what Phelana would say if he did these things. The woman had placed her trust in him, after all, and he felt he was about to violate it.

But part of him felt sure that she felt the same way he did. And in the end, that was the part that won.

Chapter Twelve

KIRK WASN'T ANGRY with Gary Mitchell anymore. In fact, Mitchell was the farthest thing from his mind.

The lieutenant gazed at Phelana as she lay beside him, his covers pulled up to the magical sweep of her collarbone, her silver hair spread out in a fan on his pillow. She was asleep, but he couldn't join her. He was too moved by the nearness of her, too staggered by the turn of events that had brought her to his bed.

Sleep, he mused, just wasn't an option.

As if she had suddenly become aware that Kirk was staring at her, Phelana's ebony eyes opened and fixed on him, and her antennae bowed in his direction. "It's almost morning," she told him softly.

"So it is."

"You've got to get some rest."

He shook his head slowly, appreciatively. "No, I don't."

The Andorian smiled. "Yes, you do. You're the helmsman, aren't you?"

"I can steer this ship with my eyes closed."

"No doubt," Phelana replied. "Still, I think I speak for everyone when I say I'd rather you didn't try."

The lieutenant smiled, too. "All right, then," he said, tracing her cheekbone with his fingertips, entranced by the way her eyelashes seemed to flutter in response. "I'll—"

His quip was cut short by the sound of a feminine voice blaring over the intercom system. "This is Commander Mangione," it said with an unmasked sense of urgency. "All cadets are to report to their quarters immediately and remain there until further notice."

Kirk looked at his companion. Her brow was creased and her antennae were standing up straight—signs that she was as surprised and confused about the order as he was.

"I repeat," said the first officer. "All cadets are to report to their quarters and remain there until further notice. Mangione out."

"What's going on?" Phelana asked.

"Damned if I know," the lieutenant told her. "I've never heard Mangione issue that kind of command."

Abruptly, another voice made itself heard over the intercom. "Jim?" it said. "Are you awake?"

Kirk bit his lip. Of all the people he didn't want to hear from right now . . .

Phelana looked at him. "Who . . . ?"

"Cadet Mitchell," he told her in a whisper. Then he raised his voice. "What is it?"

Mitchell didn't respond to the question right away. "Did I hear you speaking to someone?" he asked.

Kirk frowned. "That's none of your business and you know it. Now, what can I do for you?"

"There is someone with you," the underclassman concluded in a gleeful voice. "Good for you, you old fox."

The lieutenant glanced apologetically at Phelana. "Last chance, Cadet. Was there something you wanted to talk about?"

"You're not kidding there's something I want to talk about. Didn't you hear Mangione's orders?"

"I heard them," Kirk confirmed.

"And aren't you the least bit curious about them?" Mitchell wondered.

"Of course I am," the upperclassman replied, "for all the good it's likely to do me. If Bannock had wanted us to know what was happening, he would have made sure to tell us."

"But you're a lieutenant, for godsakes. The man's bound to let you in on this thing eventually."

"To you," said Kirk, "I'm a lieutenant. To Captain Bannock, I'm just another lowly cadet."

"I don't believe that," said Mitchell.

The lieutenant sighed. "He confined me to quarters, didn't he? Just like the rest of you?"

There was a pause. "So you're just going to accept this? You're going to go on as if nothing happened?"

"It's probably not that big a deal," Kirk told him. What's more, he believed it. "Some kind of maneuvers or something. If I were you, I'd go back to sleep."

"Easy for you to say, pal. You've got somebody to keep you warm."

The lieutenant felt his cheeks burning with embarrassment. "Sleep, Mitchell. That's an order."

He could hear the faint click of the intercom system disengaging. Shaking his head, he turned to Phelana.

"Sorry about that," he told her.

She shrugged. "It's not your fault." As she gazed at him, her eyes seemed to lose their focus.

"What is it?" Kirk asked, sensing that something was bothering her. *Dammit,* he thought, *if Mitchell's ruined this for me . . .*

The Andorian frowned. "You know, I don't blame your friend. I'm a little curious about what happened tonight myself."

The lieutenant brought his face closer to hers, drinking in the perfume of her skin and her platinum hair. "And I guess there's nothing I can do to take your mind off it."

Phelana grinned playfully. "I'm not sure I'd say that, exactly. . . ."

It seemed to Mitchell that he had just drifted off to sleep when he heard the first officer's voice fill his quarters again.

"This is Commander Mangione," the woman said. "All cadets are free to move about the ship and resume their duties. I repeat . . . all cadets are free to move about the ship and resume their duties. Mangione out."

Thanks a lot, Mitchell thought sourly.

Growing up, he had always hated kids who kept secrets from other kids—him, in particular. Now Bannock and his officers had done the same thing to him. He had applied to the Academy so he could plumb the deepest mysteries of the universe, not remain chained to his bed while Starfleet added some mysteries of its own.

Worse, there was no way he could go back to sleep now. Having been woken up twice already, his body was too ready for a third time. Acknowledging the fact, he swung his legs out of bed and sat up.

A glance at the chronometer told him it was later than he had thought. *How about that,* he mused. *I would have woken up in a few minutes anyway.*

So why do I feel so lousy? he asked himself. *Could it be because I've been tossing and turning ever since Mangione made her announcement? Could it be because my brain's been buzzing all night, trying its best to figure out what Bannock was up to?*

Yeah, he thought, answering his own question. *It sure could be.*

Getting up, the cadet made his way to the bathroom. Once he arrived there, he showered and shaved. Then he threw on a fresh gold-and-black uniform and made his way out into the corridor, hoping to find a clue or two to what had gone on during the night.

Just as Mitchell emerged from his quarters, he saw

the Andorian woman he had admired in the lounge the day before. She was coming out of a door just down the hall. But it wasn't her door, he realized.

It was Kirk's.

Kirk's . . . ?

As the plebe considered this, the Andorian glanced over her shoulder and caught sight of him. For a moment, their eyes met and they just stared at each other, wondering what might come next.

After all, she seemed to know that he was Kirk's friend—and now, just as surely, he knew that she had a stake in the lieutenant as well. Mitchell smiled in recognition of the situation.

After a second's hesitation, the woman smiled back at him. Then she turned around and walked away, headed for whatever assignment the captain had seen fit to give her.

Will wonders never cease, the underclassman mused approvingly. *Not only does that devil Jim Kirk wangle a girlfriend, he snares the prettiest woman on the ship.*

He had barely completed the thought when the lieutenant himself emerged from his quarters . . . only to find his friend leering at him. He reddened, then walked over to Mitchell and spoke confidentially as other cadets passed them in either direction.

"Whatever you're thinking," he said in little more than a whisper, "whatever off-color comment is brewing in your cesspool of a brain, I'd be grateful if you kept it to yourself."

Mitchell pretended his feelings had been hurt. "Is that what you think of me? After all we've been through together?"

Kirk looked at him. "Unless I missed something, we haven't been through anything together. And we're not going to get the chance to go through anything together if you wreck my relationship with Phelana, because I'm going to kill you the first chance I get."

The underclassman nodded. "I see. This is serious, then?"

"It could be."

Mitchell could sympathize with that. "All right. I mean, it's my nature to interfere, but I promise not to screw it up for you. And maybe you can do something for me in return."

The lieutenant seemed to have an idea what that might be. "You want me to find out what happened last night."

"That's exactly right."

"But I told you," said Kirk, "I can't."

The plebe shook his head. "What you said was Bannock wouldn't tell you. But there are other ways to find things out."

The lieutenant looked at him askance. "Such as?"

"Leave that to me," Mitchell told him.

"I don't like the sound of that."

"And I don't like being kept in the dark," said the underclassman. "See you after first shift."

Leaving a frowning Kirk standing there in the corridor, Mitchell walked away. He was halfway to the forward weapons center, where he would be working that day, when a plan began to formulate in his mind.

He chuckled to himself just thinking about it.

* * *

Kirk stared at his friend Mitchell. "Are you out of your mind?" he asked with utter sincerity.

They were standing in the anteroom of Mitchell's quarters, where no one in the corridor outside could eavesdrop on them. Still, the lieutenant didn't want to raise his voice any more than he had to.

The underclassman shrugged. "I thought we'd established that fact a long time ago."

"I'm serious," said Kirk, in no mood for jokes.

"So am I," his friend responded. "And if we do this right, no one needs to be the wiser."

The lieutenant shook his head emphatically. "You don't get it, do you? We're not talking about just another prank here, like the one you pulled with the helm monitor."

"We're talking about an action with potentially serious consequences," Mitchell shot back. "Don't you think I know that?"

"One wouldn't think so," Kirk remarked.

"Dammit," said the underclassman, "so I'm taking a chance. Taking chances is what life is all about, Jim. It's what going out into space in a metal shell is all about."

"That's different," said Kirk.

"Is it?" asked Mitchell. "If you don't learn to take risks now, you may never learn. You'll wind up in some first officer's chair and play it safe all the time, and never live up to all that potential everybody says you have."

The lieutenant felt the sting of that last remark—just as his friend had no doubt intended. Still, he kept his feet on the ground.

"Being a captain isn't about gambling," he pointed out. "It's about sound, rational decision making."

"When you're lucky," Mitchell countered. "But what happens when there are no rational decisions left to make? What happens when none of your choices are safe ones?"

Kirk shrugged the question away. "I suppose I'll cross that bridge when I come to it."

"That's probably what General Korrgar said before his defeat at Donatu Five."

That caught the lieutenant off-guard. "What?"

"Korrgar, the commander in chief of the Klingon forces. He cursed his inability to improvise on the field of battle, attributing it to the rigid principles he had been taught by his military elders."

The underclassman was right. Korrgar *had* made the comment . . . just prior to issuing the self-destruct order that annihilated his ship and crew. But how the blazes . . . ?

"I read on ahead," Mitchell confessed. "Don't look so suprised. After all, those who do not learn from history are doomed to be embarrassed in class by their instructor."

As angry as he was, Kirk was tempted to smile. He resisted the impulse. "I'm glad I made an impression on you."

"Yes," said the other man, "but the question is . . . have *I* made an impression on *you?*"

To his surprise, the lieutenant found himself wavering ever so slightly. It scared him. Sure, Korrgar's comment was a powerful argument for taking chances. But the Klingon had been talking about life and death. Mitchell was just trying to satisfy his curiosity.

"You make a good case," Kirk said at last. "But this isn't Donatu Five. All that hangs in the balance is some privileged information that probably wouldn't interest us anyway."

The underclassman's nostrils flared. "And you can't justify risking your career for that," he added.

"In a nutshell, no."

Mitchell nodded. "Okay. Sorry I brought it up."

The lieutenant eyed him suspiciously. "That's it?" he asked, waiting for the other shoe to drop.

"That's it, pal. I gave it my best shot and you turned me down. Period, end of story."

Kirk chuckled nervously. "I don't think so," he said. "You're still going through with it, aren't you?"

Mitchell returned his scrutiny. "What business is that of yours?"

"You made it my business."

"And if I *were* planning to go through with it? What would you do . . . report me to Bannock?"

The lieutenant swallowed. He wasn't sure he was prepared to betray his friend. But if he let Mitchell pursue his plan alone, he would almost certainly get caught . . . and wouldn't that be another form of betrayal?

There was a third option open to him, of course. A way to ensure that his friend wouldn't get caught. In the beginning, it had seemed like the most onerous course of action, the one tack Kirk wasn't prepared to take.

But the more he thought about it . . . the more he

considered what Mitchell would do in his place, were their positions reversed . . . the more justifiable it seemed to him.

"Well?" the underclassman prompted.

"Quiet," said Kirk, having resigned himself to his fate. "I'm trying to plan our getaway."

Mitchell looked at him for a moment. Then he smiled. "Welcome aboard, Lieutenant. It's going to be a hell of a ride."

As Mitchell rested the back of his head against the wall of the lift compartment, he acknowledged an insistent ache behind the bridge of his nose. But then, he always felt that way when he missed too much sleep.

The night before, Commander Mangione had woken him with her announcement that all cadets had to stay in their quarters. And after that, of course, he had been unable to fall into a deep sleep again.

But the plebe couldn't blame tonight's missed slumber on Mangione. This was entirely his own idea . . . this waking up in the wee hours to sneak down the corridor and slip into an empty turbolift, which could then carry him to his ultimate destination.

After all, if he was to be successful in his mission, it was important that he execute it when most of the crew was in bed. Mitchell had believed that from the beginning—and once his accomplice had joined in the plot, he had thought so too.

Abruptly, the lift doors opened. The cadet roused himself and took a peek outside. The corridor was empty.

He turned to his confederate. "Ready?"

Kirk took a breath. "Ready."

Together, they emerged from the turbolift, made a left, and followed the curve of the corridor. Before too long, it brought them to a set of sliding doors. The sign to one side of them identified the facility beyond them as the sensor control room.

Mitchell looked around. There was no one in sight, no one to question them or wonder what they were doing. Just as he had hoped.

"Here goes nothing," he said.

The plebe approached the doors and watched them open for him. They revealed a room about four meters square, with overhead lighting that picked out tiny iridescences in the duranium bulkheads.

There was only one piece of equipment in the room—a large, gray bank of controls that vaguely resembled a transporter console, but was actually the ship's main sensor board. In a way, it was a little disappointing. Mitchell had expected something more imposing, more impressive, considering it ran every bit of sensor equipment on the *Republic*.

"Come on," said the underclassman, leading the way inside.

Kirk took a last look around, satisfied himself that there were no witnesses present, and followed Mitchell in. A moment later, the doors slid closed behind them.

Working quickly, Mitchell brought up the sensor logs for the night before, knowing they would go a long way toward telling them what they wanted to know. At the same time, Kirk punched in security-baffling sequences that would cover their tracks instantly, ensuring that no one on the bridge would be aware of their intrusion.

If someone happened coincidentally to run a diagnostic, they might detect a glitch in the system, but they wouldn't suspect it was two cadets sticking their noses in Starfleet business. And by the time they got down there to check it out, Mitchell and Kirk would be gone.

Anyway, that was the plan.

"What's taking so long?" asked the lieutenant.

The underclassman spared him a glance. "Nothing. I'm getting it."

"Get it faster," Kirk urged him.

"Your wish," said Mitchell, "is my command." He turned to the blue screen near the center of the console. "Here we go."

A moment later, the screen lit up. But, to the underclassman's surprise, it had nothing on it. No graphics, no text . . . no information at all.

He stared at it, dumbfounded. "I don't get it."

"You must have done something wrong," the lieutenant told him.

Mitchell shook his head. "I don't think so. Unless . . ."

The alternative occurred to them at the same time. "They've erased the logs," said Kirk.

It was an extreme measure—a measure Bannock and his staff would never have undertaken unless they were concealing something so vital, so sensitive, they couldn't take the least chance of its being discovered.

Mitchell swallowed. He hadn't anticipated this.

Cursing sharply under his breath, he deactivated the monitor as quickly as he could. Then he turned to his companion.

"Come on," he said. "Let's get the hell out of here."

Kirk didn't answer, but his expression was desperate. Clearly, he wanted to be out of there as much as Mitchell did. Maybe more, considering everything he had to lose if he was caught.

Naturally, the doors seemed to take an eternity to open for them. Finally, they began to slide aside, giving the cadets access to the passage outside. Unable to wait any longer, they slipped through the opening sideways.

But before they could go anywhere, before the cadets could even draw another breath, they realized they weren't alone in the passageway. In fact, the underclassman thought, they were surrounded.

The barrel-chested Commander Rodianos was blocking the corridor to the right of them, while the unusually solemn-looking Chief Brown occupied the corridor to the left.

For a second or two, no one spoke. But then, no one had to. Clearly, Mitchell and his friend had been caught dead to rights, with no hope of concealing the fact.

Finally, it was Rodianos who broke the silence. "I believe Captain Bannock would like a word with you two," he said.

Chapter Thirteen

MITCHELL STOOD beside his friend Kirk in the *Republic*'s briefing room, his chin thrust out, and endured Captain Bannock's iron stare. The man was seated across from them, his leathery face as dark and foreboding as the underbelly of a threatening storm cloud.

"Frankly," said Bannock, his voice taut with indignation, "I expected this kind of insubordination from Mr. Mitchell here."

Thanks, the cadet replied inwardly. *I love you, too.*

The captain turned to the other cadet, his eyes like ice chips. "But not from you, Lieutenant."

Kirk flinched a little. He looked as if he had been lashed with a cat o' nine tails.

"What have you got to say for yourself?" asked Bannock, ignoring Mitchell for the moment.

The muscles rippled in the lieutenant's jaw. "I . . . tender no excuse for my actions, sir."

Inwardly, Mitchell smiled. Kirk had had his chance to shunt the blame onto the plebe and he had resisted the temptation to do so.

"No excuse?" the captain rumbled, fixing the upperclassman on the spit of his glare. "No explanation, either?"

Kirk shrugged. "I made a bad decision, sir. I let my curiosity get the better of me and I regret it."

Bannock glanced at Mitchell, though he was still speaking to the lieutenant. "The way I see it, Mr. Kirk, you were trying to help a friend. Is that a fair assessment of the situation?"

Mitchell frowned. The captain was giving the upperclassman a second opportunity to deflect blame—a second shot at walking away with an unblemished record. But if he knew Kirk, the man would stand his ground.

A moment later, the lieutenant shook his head. "Not at all, sir," he said. "I acted entirely of my own free will."

Attaboy, the plebe cheered within the privacy of his mind. *Show the bastard what you're made of.*

The captain turned back to Kirk and scrutinized him for a while. Then he harrumphed disapprovingly.

"The truth, Lieutenant—and we all know it—is you did try to help a friend. And you're trying to help him still. But let me tell you, Mr. Kirk . . . in this case, your loyalty is misplaced."

Bannock darted a look at the underclassman that would have melted a glacier. "Cadet Mitchell," he said, "is not your friend. He's a plebe, and a very irresponsible one at that. The more time you spend with this man, the more you learn from him, the further you'll get from that captain's chair you seem to covet."

That one hurt, thought Mitchell. He could tell by the way Kirk's eyes narrowed, by the way his lips pressed together.

Still, the lieutenant didn't cave in. He remained utterly silent, enduring the punishment of Bannock's remarks.

"Nothing to say on the subject?" asked the captain.

A third opportunity, Mitchell noted. Clearly, the captain wanted desperately to let Kirk off the hook. But as before, the lieutenant didn't seem eager to cooperate.

"Nothing at all?" Bannock prodded.

"Nothing I haven't already said, sir," Kirk replied. There was no rancor in his voice, no insolence. Just an unwavering resolve.

Bannock sat back in his chair and drummed his fingers on the table beside him. "You know," he told the lieutenant, "I should send a message to your commandant and tell him what you've done. That would effectively put an end to any hope you had of a career."

Mitchell's heart sank in sympathy. He could only imagine what his friend was going through.

"But," the captain went on in the same tone of voice, "I've decided not to do that. For some reason I can't quite figure out, I'm inclined to give you a second chance."

Kirk looked grateful.

"See that you don't blow it," said Bannock.

The lieutenant nodded. "I won't, sir."

"Thank you, sir," Mitchell added.

The captain glanced at him. "You *should* thank me, Cadet. You should thank me from the bottom of your heart."

But the plebe didn't feel the least bit grateful. He knew that if he had been caught in the sensor room alone, his career would have been over before it began.

What had saved him was Kirk's involvement in the incident. Bannock couldn't bust Mitchell without busting the lieutenant as well, and he was obviously reluctant to do that.

The captain regarded the cadets for a cold second or two longer. Then he said, "Dismissed. Both of you."

Mitchell turned around with a bit more alacrity, so he got to the briefing-room door a little quicker. A moment later, Kirk followed, and the door whispered shut behind them.

Taking a deep breath, Mitchell glanced at his friend. "Thanks for standing up for me in there."

Kirk returned the glance. "Standing up for you?"

"You know," said the underclassman, "sharing the blame . . . and ignoring Bannock's invitations to cut me loose."

The lieutenant's expression changed. "You know," he said, "I'm not so sure the captain was wrong."

Mitchell looked at him. "What?"

"What we did was stupid," Kirk told him, his eyes hard and angry. "It was worse than stupid—it was childish. If Bannock didn't want us to know something, we should have taken a hint."

Mitchell shook his head wonderingly. "You're serious, aren't you?"

The lieutenant nodded. "Damned right I'm serious. And just so you know, I do want to be a captain someday. I want to command a starship just like this one. That's why I can't afford anything . . . or anyone . . . that might throw me off that course."

"Meaning me?" the plebe wondered.

Kirk's mouth twisted. "Meaning you."

Without another word, the lieutenant turned his back and walked away, leaving Mitchell standing all alone in the corridor.

The underclassman felt a lump forming in his throat. He had begun to consider Jim Kirk a friend and a confidant. Obviously, he had overestimated the man—overestimated him greatly.

But then, as the lieutenant himself had pointed out, even a guy with "intuition" could make mistakes.

Kirk lay on his back, his hands tucked behind his head, and replayed the scene outside the briefing room over and over in his mind. He could see himself glaring at Mitchell, angry that he had let himself be sucked into the other man's scheme.

What we did was stupid, he heard himself say. *It was worse than stupid—it was childish.*

Lying beside him, Phelana ran her slender fingernails across the skin of his naked chest. Under different circumstances, Kirk thought, the sensation would have been a most pleasant one. As it was, he found himself frowning at the distraction.

And just so you know, the upperclassman heard himself continue, *I do want to be a captain someday. I want to command a starship just like this one. That's why I can't afford anything . . . or anyone . . . that might throw me off that course.*

They were hard words. Cruel words, maybe. But then, he had intended them to be cruel. He had meant to cut himself off from his friend as surely and irrevocably as he could.

"He'll understand someday," Phelana said softly. "He'll see it was all for the best."

Kirk shook his head. "No, he won't."

"Come on," she insisted. "We're all here to build careers in Starfleet. No one wants to go home in disgrace."

The lieutenant sighed. "Mitchell is different. He doesn't give a damn what happens to him."

His companion looked at him askance. "He has no ambition? No dreams of commanding a starship someday?"

"None," said Kirk. "He's not the ambitious kind. He's just in Starfleet for the fun of it."

Phelana smiled a bit uncertainly. "You're joking, right?"

He shook his head. "Not a bit."

The Andorian pondered the information, her antennae bending forward. "Then maybe he doesn't belong here after all."

Kirk looked at her, ready to argue the contrary. Then he saw the wisdom in Phelana's words.

"Maybe he doesn't," he conceded.

Mitchell didn't see Kirk even once over the next couple of days. On a ship the size of the Constitution-class *Republic,* which was built to handle hundreds of crewmen and still have room for amenities, that didn't come as a real surprise to him.

Then the ship came in sensor range of Alpha Varangis, the first star system on her survey swing. Mitchell and Kirk were both assigned to the science station on the bridge—and while they worked different shifts, they still saw each other coming and going each day.

It didn't change anything. The lieutenant didn't say a word to the underclassman, and the underclassman didn't say a word to the lieutenant. It was as if they didn't know each other . . . which seemed to be exactly the way Kirk wanted it.

Mitchell didn't like the idea that he and the lieutenant would never be friends again, but he could accept it. Life, he had learned, was like that. You win a few, you lose a few.

However, his obligation to Kirk went beyond mere friendship. He had assumed responsibility for the upperclassman's personal development, no matter how frivolously at first, and it irked him that a stuffed shirt like Bannock was preventing him from carrying out his mission.

If nothing else, Mitchell wanted to have the last laugh on his commanding officer. If he saw a chance to do that, he told himself, he would take advantage of it . . . in a heartbeat.

Unfortunately, that chance didn't come during their three-day survey of Alpha Varangis. Everyone did his or her job and everything went according to plan. It was only as they were about to leave the system that Bannock changed everything with a surprise announcement.

"We've got new orders," he told cadets and command officers alike, standing before them in the ship's lounge.

"What kind?" asked Mangione.

"Apparently," said the captain, "Captain Nakamura and his ship were supposed to represent the Federation at a diplomatic event. However, the *Carolina* has been assigned something described to me as 'more critical duties,' leaving the task of representing the Federation to guess who."

"Us?" Rodianos replied, straight-faced.

"You guessed it," Bannock answered, equally straight-faced. He included the cadets in a single glance. "No doubt, it would have been more educational for you to continue our survey course, but it's not as if we've got a choice in the matter."

"Where are we going?" asked Gorfinkel, echoing the question on Mitchell's mind.

"A place called Heir'tzan," the captain told him. "It's in the Beta Bora system. Maybe you've heard of it."

Brown stroked his beard for a moment. "A member world, isn't it? Newly inducted?"

Bannock nodded. "Along with its sister world, Heir'ocha."

"How cozy," said the engineer, smiling his ear-to-ear smile.

The captain eyed him. "Actually, Lieutenant, there's nothing cozy about it. These two worlds have a history."

Gorfinkel grunted. "Not a good one, I take it."

"Not a good one at all," Bannock agreed. "Once, it seems, there were two groups of Heiren on Heir'tzan. But a little more than two hundred years ago, both groups decided they could no longer stand each other's company. One faction—the one that called itself the Heir'och—abandoned its homeworld and took up residence on a neighboring planet."

"That would be Heir'ocha?" asked Hogan.

"It would," said the captain. "At first, the Heir'och's departure was just fine with the other faction, which called itself the Heir'tza. After all, they had their homeworld to themselves all of a sudden, free of bickering. But before long, the Heir'och and the Heir'tza were finding new reasons to bump heads . . . economic, cultural, and even religious reasons.

"Despite the distance between them, the situation grew more and more volatile, more and more tumultuous. Eventually, it flared into an interplanetary war, which was waged on and off for nearly a century. A bloody, savage thing, as I understand it."

Aren't they all? Mitchell wondered. But he refrained from posing the question out loud.

"Even after a truce was declared," said Bannock, "bad feelings prevailed for decades. Blood feuds claimed victim after victim, sparking new blood feuds. And both planets remained armed camps, ready to explode at the first sign of treachery.

"It was only over the last fifty years or so that elements of both factions began trying to bring their people together again." The captain frowned. "Unfortunately, their efforts were undermined by hatred and mistrust. They kept taking one step forward and two steps back."

"I have seen that dance before," said Tarsch, his words slurred and garbled by the obtrusive presence of his Vobilite tusks. "It is never a very pleasant thing to behold."

"No, it's not," the captain agreed. "Eventually, even the strongest proponents of Heiren reconciliation began to think their efforts weren't amounting to anything."

"I'm not surprised," said Gorfinkel.

"Then," Bannock continued, "someone found an answer to the problem. It was in the Heiren gene pool, of all places. You see, the Heiren species had produced a powerful telepath or two in every generation, as far back as anyone could remember."

That got Mitchell's attention. After all, his flashes of insight were a distant cousin to telepathy. Or so he'd always believed.

"Such an individual," said Bannock, "could help his or her faction cut through the mistrust. He could read the minds of the other side and get a sense of their intentions. Unfortunately, that would only help the faction to which the telepath belonged. The other one would still be operating very much in the dark."

"Unless both factions produced a telepath," Mangione suggested.

"Exactly," the captain responded. "Two telepaths would ensure honest relations between the Heir'tza and the Heir'och—and a reconciliation couldn't help but be far behind. Or so the theory went.

"Three generations later, the Heiren finally have an opportunity to put their theory to the test. Each side has produced a full-fledged telepath. Respected voices among both the Heir'tza and the Heir'och are saying it's time for their species to come together again."

Tarsch tilted his head. "You sound skeptical."

Bannock shrugged. "Frankly, Doctor, it's none of my business whether these telepaths are the answer or not. My job—and yours—is to apply some Starfleet expertise to the proceedings."

"Which you've yet to describe," Rodianos reminded him.

The captain rewarded him with a crinkling of the skin around the corners of his mouth. It was as close as Mitchell had ever seen the captain come to a bona fide smile.

"I'm getting to that," Bannock said. "Now, from what the Heiren tell us, this is the way it's supposed to work. . . ."

According to age-old Heiren custom, Bannock explained, all signatories to an important pact were supposed to prove their good intentions by showing themselves in a public place. In accordance with that custom, the two telepaths would make their appearance on Heir'tzan, in the bustling capital city of Heir'at.

"There are two ancient temples in town," the captain said. "Each telepath will show up at one of them. Then, at a preappointed time, they'll take off their shoes and approach one another along the city's main thoroughfare, allowing everyone to get a good look at them.

"Eventually," Bannock pointed out, "the telepaths will come together at the Heir'tzan government building. Since the place is equidistant from the two temples, they should arrive there at the same time. And the rest, as they say, will be history."

Brown shrugged. "Sounds simple."

Mitchell thought so, too.

"It's not," Bannock told the engineer. "Understand, not everyone on both sides wants this event to take place."

"Those blood feuds," Mangione reminded them.

"Exactly," said the captain. "From what I'm told, some people may be willing to spill blood to nip the ceremony in the bud. And given the archaic bent of the Heiren and the rigid nature of their ceremonies, they'll probably have plenty of opportunity."

Rodianos leaned forward on his chair. "Tell me more."

"Spoken like a true security officer," said Bannock. He rubbed the palms of his hands together in a way Mitchell found vaguely annoying. "Apparently, each temple is more than a kilometer from the government building. That leaves our telepaths vulnerable for a good, long time. The capital is heavily populated to begin with, and it'll be even more mobbed during this historic event, so you can forget about any attempts at crowd control."

"I'll say," Mangione remarked.

"To compound the problem," the captain went on, "the temples can't be closed to their congregations at any time, so the telepaths have to be hidden elsewhere until the moment the ceremony begins. Several sites will be selected and guarded—though only two of them will actually be used as hiding places. The rest will serve as decoys."

Brown shook his head. "Tougher and tougher."

"Finally," Bannock told them, "in the name of Heiren tradition, no one in the city is allowed to use modern technology—not even the people charged with guarding the telepaths. That means no phasers, no communicators, no beaming in or out."

Silence reigned. It was Kirk who broke it.

"Will the Heir'tza—or for that matter, the Heir'och—hurt a telepath from their own faction?" he asked.

"Good question," said Bannock. "I'm told they'll stop short of inflicting bodily harm on their own faction's telepath . . . but they may not have a problem with kidnapping him."

"Which," Rodianos noted judiciously, "would be only slightly more difficult under such circumstances."

The captain nodded. "To tell you the truth, I'm not thrilled about the whole thing. Our crew isn't up to this kind of mission. We don't have the training or the experience. However, I've been assured by Command that we'll only shoulder part of the responsibility for security. Most of it will fall to our Heir'tza hosts."

"So what will we be doing, exactly?" asked Gorfinkel.

Bannock told them. Of course, Mitchell didn't pay much attention to what the man was saying until his name came up.

"Cadets Kirk, Yudrin, and Mitchell," said the captain, "will be assigned to help out at the bakery."

The underclassman wasn't sure he had heard Bannock correctly. "I beg your pardon, sir?"

The captain focused on him and him alone. "The bakery, Mr. Mitchell. I assume you know what a bakery is?"

The cadet could feel his cheeks flushing. "Yes, sir," he replied as calmly as he could, "I believe I do."

"Good," said Bannock. "The bakery in this case is an ancient structure not far from one of the temples. It's also one of the places where one of the telepaths may be hidden until the time of the ceremony." He eyed Kirk, then Phelana, then Mitchell. "I hope you all understand the importance of maintaining security in this building?"

"Aye, sir," Kirk answered.

"Absolutely, sir," said Phelana.

Mitchell didn't like being treated like a child. "It's where the telepath may be hidden, sir. As you just said, sir."

Bannock glared at him, out didn't take the bait.

"I'm told there will be plenty of Heir'tza guards in and around the place. But don't let them do all the work. Pull your weight, just as you would anywhere else."

"And if there's trouble?" asked Mangione.

The captain grunted. "You're to defer to the Heir'tza security officer in charge. And under no circumstances whatsoever are you to leave the vicinity of the bakery. Is that clear?"

"Clear, sir," said Kirk.

"Very clear, sir," replied Phelana.

Mitchell hesitated. "Under *no* circumstances, sir?"

"That's correct," said Bannock.

The plebe wondered about the wisdom of that. "Even if it directly bears on the success or failure of our mission?"

The captain's mouth became a thin, straight line. "Are you making an effort to try my patience, Cadet?"

"No, sir," Mitchell answered honestly. "I was just trying to understand your orders, sir."

"In that case, I'll say it again. Under no circumstances are you to leave the vicinity of the bakery. No circumstances at all. Do you understand my orders now, Cadet?"

Mitchell wanted to tell the captain how little he cared for the man's tone. However, he managed to keep a lid on his feelings. "I do, sir."

"You're sure?" asked Bannock.

"I'm sure, sir," said the underclassman.

"Good," said the captain, pulling down on the

front of his tunic. "I'll sleep much better knowing that."

Kirk lingered outside the briefing room until Mitchell came out. When the other cadet saw him standing there, he walked right by him, seemingly oblivious of the lieutenant's existence.

The upperclassman wasn't surprised. After all, he and Mitchell hadn't spoken for nearly a week—and it was Kirk, after all, who was responsible for that state of affairs.

But whether he liked it or not, they had to talk now.

"Mitchell," said the lieutenant.

The other cadet stopped and turned to him, a look of suppressed resentment on his face. "Yes, sir?"

Kirk frowned. "Listen," he said, "I don't know why the captain threw us together any more than you do. What I do know is we've got a mission to carry out. That's got to come first. The mission—not what's taken place between you and me."

Mitchell quirked a smile. "All right. I'll buy that."

The lieutenant nodded. "Just so we understand each other."

"That we do," said the younger man. Then, with a look that accused, he walked away.

Kirk swore beneath his breath. He hadn't wanted to cast Mitchell aside like an old shoe. He hadn't wanted to hurt the man's feelings.

But it would have meant his career if he had gone on being friends with the underclassman. It would have meant disappointing not only himself, but also Captain April and Admiral Mallory.

And, no matter what, he had promised himself he wouldn't do that.

"Jim?" said a feminine voice.

The lieutenant saw that Phelana had joined him. "Mm?"

"Is everything all right?" she asked.

He watched Mitchell negotiate a bend in the hallway and disappear from view. "Fine," he told her, "just fine."

Chapter Fourteen

To Kirk, the Heir'tza capital looked liked a fairy-tale kingdom—a place that had been plucked out of the Arabian Nights book his mother used to read to him when he was a boy.

Standing beside a high, narrow window, the lieutenant gazed at the splendor of Heir'at's skyline. It was morning, a couple of hours past dawn, and the city's tall, narrow towers and teardrop-shaped roofs shone furiously in the brazen sunlight.

Flimsy green and blue pennants fluttered on high, arching streetlamps. Balloons painted in iridescent colors rose from weighted baskets on every corner. Scarlet and silver banners, draped from window to window, proclaimed the beginning of an age of trust and harmony.

It was a time of great optimism for the Heir'tza—

this world's scaly, bronze-skinned inhabitants—and their equally scaly brethren, the Heir'och. Members of both factions had festooned themselves with all manner of finery to celebrate the reunion of their peoples.

Kirk could see them from his vantage point on the second floor of the bakery—one of Heir'at's most ancient buildings, apparently. The Heiren in the streets below him looked so exuberant, so festive, it was difficult to imagine there might be dissidents in their midst—people ruthless and coldhearted enough to commit murder if it meant throwing a monkey wrench into the telepaths' reconciliation ceremony.

Of course, if the dissidents could smell what the lieutenant was smelling at the moment, they would forget all about the ceremony. In fact, they might forget their own names.

After all, the ovens in the basement two floors below him were working overtime to satisfy the celebratory needs of the Heir'tza, filling the rest of the building with the rich, buttery aroma of doughy pastries sweltering on hot stones. Just thinking about it made Kirk's stomach growl.

Phelana leaned closer to him. "I know one of the telepaths could be hidden downstairs," she commented sotto voce, "but it's going to be difficult to concentrate on anything but that smell."

"It already is," he told her.

Apparently, the bakery's fragrance was having a similar effect on the Heir'tza security operatives who shared the meeting room with them. Their yellow eyes had narrowed to slits and their pointed ears were lying flat against their long, hairless skulls.

Mitchell must have been enjoying the smell, too. But he wasn't saying anything about it. In fact, he hadn't said anything about anything since the three cadets had transported from the *Republic* to the planet's surface a half hour earlier.

The lieutenant sighed, wishing things had turned out differently, wishing he and the underclassman could have remained friends. For one thing, it would have made this mission a lot less uncomfortable for them.

And for Phelana as well. Unlike Kirk, she barely knew Mitchell, but the plebe wasn't speaking to her any more than he had to. Guilt by association, the lieutenant mused.

Just as the thought crossed his mind, Ar Bintor walked into the room. The Second Minister of Security for Heir'at was a squat, bowlegged fellow with thick, muscular arms and legs and a brow ridge any Heir'tza would have been proud of.

The assembled security operatives gave the fellow their undivided attention. Despite the allure of the smells wafting up from below, Kirk tried his best to do the same.

"I know you've all been briefed in advance," said Bintor, "but let me tell you again how important this operation is. What happens on the streets of Heir'at today can lead to the kind of peace our forefathers could only dream about—or it could just as easily lead to war and bloodshed. The outcome is entirely up to us."

A murmur of acknowledgment ran through the ranks of the Heir'tza. Kirk and his fellow cadets just nodded.

"Some of you may be tempted to relax," the minister continued. "After all, none of us knows where the telepaths are hidden, myself included, and this is only one of several possible locations. Nonetheless, I will demand the utmost vigilance of you—for if one of the telepaths is hidden here, and we allow him to be captured or killed, we will be branded villains and worse for many years to come."

Kirk didn't doubt it. What's more, he had no intention of being branded a villain or worse, especially when his behavior on Heir'tzan reflected on the entire Federation.

"Does everyone understand his or her assignment?" asked Bintor. He looked deadly serious, his ears flared and his eyes wide and round.

Kirk didn't. He raised his hand to signify as much.

"Your pardon, Second Minister," he said, "but my colleagues and I haven't received an assignment yet."

Bintor took in the three Starfleet cadets at a glance. "You're correct, Lieutenant. I will cure the oversight immediately." He seemed to give the matter some thought. "You will establish yourselves across the street from the bakery's north wall."

"All three of us?" asked Mitchell.

"All three," the minister confirmed. Then, as if he felt that was all the cadets needed to know, he turned again to his fellow Heir'tza.

"Your pardon," Kirk said a second time, "but isn't it possible to find a better use for us?"

Bintor looked at him. "Such as?"

"I don't know," the lieutenant replied. "But you have two teams deployed along the north wall already."

The security official's chin came up. "I have two teams deployed along *every* wall."

"All the more reason," Kirk pressed, "to move us to another position. For instance, one closer to the telepaths' route."

Bintor's wide nostrils flared even wider. "My associates, the third and fourth ministers, have attended to that. In fact, we have attended to all our projected needs."

"But, sir—" the lieutenant began.

"To be blunt," the Hier'tza went on, raising his voice over the human's objection, "I see your presence here as a mere gesture on the part of your Federation. Were you not apprised of that understanding?"

Kirk frowned. "I was not, Minister. What I was told was that we would be pulling our weight, which is what we still hope to do. In fact, I thought we might start by—"

"It is not necessary for you to think," Bintor told him, his eyes flashing in his scaly, bronze countenance. He smiled a broad but humorless smile, baring small, upward-curving fangs. "It is only necessary for you to obey."

The lieutenant didn't appreciate the sentiment. On the other hand, Bannock had told him to follow the Heir'tza's directives.

174

His smile fading, the security minister turned slowly to face his native operatives. "Now," he said, "is there anyone else who has a question about his or her assignment?"

No one did.

"In that case," Ar Bintor told them, "you may disperse and report to your assigned positions."

The Heir'tza operatives began filing out of the room, followed by the security minister himself. That left the three Starfleet cadets looking at each other. Mitchell and Phelana looked frustrated.

Kirk was frustrated, too, for all the good it would do them. He shrugged, as if to say, There's nothing more I can do.

Phelana seemed to understand that. But not Mitchell. He shot the lieutenant a look of dissatisfaction.

"You heard what Bintor told me," the lieutenant declared. "As far as he's concerned, we're just window dressing."

"Hey, it's no problem at all," said the underclassman, his voice tinged with sarcasm. "I understand the street across from the north wall is nice this time of year."

And he left in the Heir'tza's wake.

Kirk bit his lip. *Damn him,* he thought.

"Mitchell's not going to make this easy for you," Phelana noted.

"I guess not," the lieutenant said.

Mitchell stood alongside his fellow cadets on a narrow street opposite the ancient bakery. Throngs of mixed Heir'tza and Heir'och flowed past them like a great, radiant river, flashing one garish color after another in the glare of the midmorning sunlight.

"Can you tell the difference between the factions?" asked Phelana.

Kirk shook his head. "I doubt the Heiren can tell the difference themselves right now."

Mitchell had to go along with that view. After all, these people were one race, one species, with a common heritage and common ancestors. Only their politics had split them in half.

Just as Kirk's politics had split his friendship with Mitchell in half. But the underclassman didn't make that comparison out loud. He put it aside and did his duty, helping to scan the crowd for anything suspicious.

Not that we're really going to spot anything, he mused. *We're too close to the crowd to have any real perspective on what's going on.*

For that matter, so were the teams of Heir'tzan guards posted up and down the street on either side of them. They gave the appearance of surveillance, but that was about it. If anything bad happened, they would be hard-pressed to catch a glimpse of it.

"This isn't working," Kirk said suddenly.

Mitchell turned to him. He wasn't surprised at how closely the lieutenant's thought mirrored his own. After all, anyone with half a brain could have come to the same conclusion. What did surprise him was Kirk's willingness to express the sentiment out loud.

"Did I hear the voice of dissent?" the plebe asked no one in particular.

Out of the corner of his eye, he could see the

lieutenant dart a look at him. "It's just an observation," Kirk told him.

"One I happen to agree with," Mitchell responded.

Then the upperclassman surprised him again. "I don't suppose you've given any thought to an alternative?"

Mitchell hadn't. But since Kirk was posing the question, he looked around—and found an option close at hand.

"What about this building?" he asked, jerking a thumb over his shoulder at the structure behind them.

Phelana looked concerned as she followed his gesture. Her antennae were straining forward, looking for all the world as if they were trying to free themselves from her head.

But it was the lieutenant who responded. "What about it?"

Mitchell shrugged. "The place looks empty, doesn't it? Maybe even abandoned. If we could get up on the roof, we'd have a much better idea of what's going on."

That was when the Andorian's concern turned into resistance. "Let's not forget—the security minister specifically assigned us this position. And Captain Bannock told us to follow the minister's orders. I don't think it would be wise to disobey either of them."

Mitchell glanced at Kirk. The upperclassman wasn't dismissing Phelana's point, but he also wasn't bowing to it.

"Bannock did tell us to follow the Heir'tza's orders," Kirk conceded. "But he also told us to make ourselves useful, and as things stand now, we're nothing more than decorations." He considered the building Mitchell had indicated. "Of course, if we stay here and something happens to one of the telepaths, no one will blame us."

The underclassman sighed. That was it, then. Once again, the lieutenant had opted for the better part of valor.

"Then again," said Kirk, still craning his neck to look at the building, *"I'll* blame us."

Phelana looked at him, stricken. "What are you saying?"

"I'm saying we need to do something," he returned. "We need to make a contribution. Otherwise, what's the point of being here at all?" And, without another word, he jogged off down the crowded street.

"Where are you going?" the Andorian demanded of him.

"To find a way up to the roof," the lieutenant called back.

Phelana shook her head, her antennae curling backward. "You can't do that. It's a direct violation of our orders."

"I'm the ranking officer here," Kirk reminded her. "If push comes to shove, you can say I demanded that you come with me."

The Andorian took a few steps after him. "But what about you? Think about your career, Jim. After what happened on the *Republic,* they could drum you right out of the Fleet for this."

It was a good point, thought Mitchell.

"Maybe they will," the lieutenant conceded, "and

maybe they won't. Right now, I can't worry about any of that. I've got to follow my instincts." He pointed to the building beside him. "And my instincts are telling me I've got to get up to the roof."

Until that moment, Mitchell had been silent . . . and rather stunned at the upperclassman's behavior. He was accustomed to the holier-than-thou Kirk, the by-the-books Kirk, the play-it-safe Kirk. This was a Kirk he had never laid eyes on before.

"Who are you," he called after the lieutenant with a straight face, "and what have you done with our fellow cadet?"

The upperclassman didn't answer. He just shot Mitchell a look of disapproval and continued his progress alongside the building, as if that were reply enough.

The Andorian hesitated for a moment, despite Kirk's invitation. Obviously, she was torn in two directions—between loyalty and duty. In the end, she opted for loyalty, and fell in behind the lieutenant at a trot.

Mitchell was only a stride behind her.

After a while, Kirk found a door in the façade of the building. Since advanced technology wasn't allowed in Heir'at, he grasped a knob and tried turning it. The door unlocked itself.

Swinging it inward, he saw that the building was dusty and dark inside. But it wasn't so dark or dusty that he couldn't make out a circular stairway a few meters away, at the end of a short hallway.

He went inside. The place echoed with the scrape of his footsteps on the plain wooden floor.

As Mitchell had surmised, the building was empty. Kirk knew that even before his eyes had adjusted to the gloom. There were no sounds of habitation, no one to stop the lieutenant as he made his way up the stairway, passing one floor after another in his ascent.

Finally, he reached a door at the top. Opening that as well, he was blinded by a flood of bright sunshine. Obviously, he had achieved his objective. He was on the roof.

He was glad to see that his comrades were right behind him. Like Kirk, they flinched at the assault of light on their eyes after the darkness within. But before long, they all managed to make their way to the roof's edge.

There, the lieutenant saw the whole of Heir'at spread out below him in elegant geometric order, each block easily distinguishable from the next. A flood of Heiren surged and roiled and eddied their way through the city's plazas and thoroughfares, looking to Kirk like a living mosaic. They caught the sun's brazen rays on their metal skullcaps and diadems, on their metal collars and brooches and their whimsically painted metal breastplates.

"This is beautiful," said Phelana, having apparently forgotten her objections to the ascent.

Kirk thought so, too. More important, from a height of five stories he and his fellow cadets could see everything that was going on below. It made him wonder why the Heir'tza hadn't adopted such a tactic themselves.

"It's beautiful, all right," Mitchell agreed. "Not to mention a damned sight less fragrant than where we were before. Nothing like a hot, perspiring mob of Heiren to make you yearn for the wide, open spaces."

The Andorian turned to him, her features screwed up in disgust. "Was that absolutely necessary?"

The underclassman shrugged. "Just calling them the way I see them, Cadet Yudrin. Or, in this case, the way I—"

"Let's not forget what we're doing here," the lieutenant interjected, cutting the two of them short. "We could do with a little less talk and a little more reconnaissance."

"Aye, sir," said Mitchell. "Whatever you—"

This time, he cut *himself* short. His brow wrinkled as he stared at something down below.

"What is it?" Kirk asked him, trying to figure out what had so riveted the underclassman's attention.

Mitchell pointed. "Look!"

The lieutenant followed the other man's gesture— and saw a Heiren body lying in an open doorway of the bakery. Judging by the splash of green on the Heiren's tunic, he was bleeding.

Bleeding, Kirk thought. As if he'd been *stabbed*.

No one in the crowd seemed to notice. And before the lieutenant could respond, the body was dragged back into the building.

"My god," Kirk said, his heart pounding in his chest.

"They're after the telepath," Phelana declared.

"And they're not taking no for an answer," Mitchell observed.

The lieutenant leaned over the edge of the roof, hoping to alert one of the security officers below. Finding a couple, he waved at them.

"Hey!" he bellowed at the top of his lungs. "Listen to me! The bakery—they've gotten inside!"

"It's no use," said Phelana, her voice taut with concern. "They can't hear you down there."

"And they're blocked off by the crowd from seeing that door," Mitchell added. "As far as they know, everything's still hunky-dory."

This isn't good, Kirk thought, wishing Heir'at's laws hadn't kept them from bringing their communicators along. *This isn't good at all. We have to get down to street level and alert Ar Bintor's people.*

But before he could move, he saw the door in the bakery open again. A festively dressed Heiren came out. Taking a quick look around, the Heiren gestured to someone behind him.

"What's going on?" asked Phelana.

A moment later, the first Heiren was joined by a half-dozen others. They filed out of the building one after the other, each of them arrayed in the same sort of celebratory finery.

Two of the Heiren shared the weight of something slung over their shoulders. It looked like a colorful, intricately woven carpet, rolled up for easier transport. But from the lieutenant's vantage point, it seemed to him there was something inside it.

Something vaguely man-shaped.

"One of the telepaths," Mitchell rasped. "He's in that carpet."

Phelana looked at him. "Are you sure?"

Mitchell returned her look. "I don't think they stabbed that guard to make off with a floor covering."

"He's right," said Kirk, surprised at how even his voice sounded all of a sudden. "It's one of the telepaths."

Moments ago, he had been frantic, his mind racing to find a way to stop the kidnapping. But now that it was a fait accompli, he felt calmer, more certain of himself somehow.

The guards down below still had no idea of what was going on. In effect, they were useless. Only the cadets were in a position to keep a bad situation from getting worse.

"We've got to stop them," Kirk said.

"We?" Phelana echoed. "But the captain's orders—"

"Didn't cover this," Mitchell told her.

The lieutenant had already come to the same conclusion. He watched the kidnappers make their way through the crowd. Unfortunately, it was four flights down to street level.

"If we take the stairs," he said, "we'll lose sight of them."

"And they'll get too much of a head start," Mitchell added. He turned to Kirk. "There's only one way to catch them."

Again, the lieutenant found himself in agreement. "One way," he echoed, grimly eyeing the ground below them.

The Andorian's eyes opened wide as she realized what they were talking about. "Oh no, you don't," she protested.

Kirk looked at her. "We've got to."

"You can't," she insisted, beseeching the lieutenant with her big, black eyes. "You'll break both your legs."

"Not if we're careful," Mitchell countered, though he didn't sound as if he was altogether sure of it himself.

Kirk frowned. "Come with us," he told Phelana.

She shook her head. "I can't, Jim."

He hesitated for a fraction of a second, not wanting to do it without her. Then he had to make a choice.

"I'm with you," Mitchell declared. But what he really meant was "Are you with me?"

The lieutenant nodded. "Let's go."

Gritting his teeth, he scanned the street directly beneath them, which was relatively clear of Heiren for the moment. Beside him, the underclassman fixed his gaze on the same spot.

"On three," said Kirk. "One. Two."

He screwed up his courage.

"Three!" he roared.

Together, he and Mitchell took a step toward the perimeter of the roof and launched themselves into the air. Legs cycling, arms extended for balance, they seemed to hover for a moment in the Heir'tzan sunlight like two big, awkward birds.

Then the street rose to meet them with an acceleration that took the lieutenant's breath away. At what seemed like the right time, he bent his legs and tried to keep his weight squarely above them.

The impact of his landing jarred his bones from his ankles to the base of his skull. It sent him stumbling face-first into the dirt. But when he picked himself up, he discovered he hadn't broken anything. In fact, he was in much better shape than he had a right to be.

Then he turned to see how Mitchell had fared. The underclassman was sitting there next to him, an expression of wonder on his face. Suddenly, he started to laugh.

"You all right?" Kirk asked him, extending a hand.

Mitchell took it and pulled himself to his feet. "Are you kidding?" he whooped. "I can't wait to go on that ride again!"

All around them, Heiren stared in wonder and remarked on the craziness of their offworld visitors. One spectator even offered to help them if they were hurt, though the lieutenant waved the fellow away.

Then he turned and looked up at Phelana. She was on her hands and knees on the edge of the roof, leaning over the brink to see how her comrades had fared. There was a distinct look of relief on her face.

One last time, Kirk beckoned to her. *Please,* he pleaded silently. *It's not too late.*

But the Andorian shook her head emphatically from side to side. *I'm staying right where I am,* she seemed to say. *If you feel you need to, then go on without me.*

The lieutenant bit his lip. Then, pulling Mitchell along with him, he plunged through the crowd in the direction he had seen the kidnappers take—and he didn't look back a second time.

Chapter Fifteen

MITCHELL HAD a feeling that he was going to regret what he had done. Even worse, he had a feeling that Kirk was going to regret it. But either way, they had come too far to back down now.

Making their way through the crowd, drawing angry stares from those they jostled to get by, they tried desperately to catch a glimpse of the telepath's abductors. Finally, Kirk pointed to something up ahead.

"I see them," he announced.

"Where?" asked Mitchell.

"About twenty meters ahead of us. Past the man with the feathered headdress."

The plebe followed Kirk's gesture and saw the carpet in which the telepath had been rolled up. "Got it."

A moment later, he caught sight of the kidnappers

as well. All seven of them were present—three in front and two in back, with the two biggest specimens carrying the telepath between them.

If they had noticed the cadets trailing them, they gave no indication of it. They didn't even seem to be in any hurry. They just moved at the pace of the crowd, a part of it like any other.

"We'll catch them in no time," Mitchell observed.

The lieutenant turned to him. "We could. But then what?"

Then what indeed, the underclassman thought. "If we accuse them in public, they could panic and kill someone."

Kirk nodded. "Maybe even the telepath."

"So what do we do?" Mitchell asked.

The other man thought for a moment. "They must have a destination in mind . . . a place where they plan on stowing their captive. We could follow them there and then alert the authorities."

The cadet watched the kidnappers shoulder their way through the crowd, toting their living cargo. "It's a deal," he said at last, unable to think of a better plan.

So as the time of the ceremony grew nearer and nearer, they pursued the telepath and his abductors from street to street . . . and hoped they had made the right choice.

Kirk wasn't surprised when the kidnappers headed for the edge of town. After all, they needed to end up as far from the site of the reconciliation ceremony as possible.

Though the dissidents looked back from time to time, they didn't seem to expect any pursuit. Even so, the cadets took pains to conceal themselves effectively, ducking into alleys and doorways and hiding behind staircases at every opportunity.

In time, they left the more crowded precincts of Heir'at behind and entered a warehouse district—an older area where the streets twisted like serpents and it became harder for Kirk to keep the kidnappers in view.

Still, they hung on to the trail, knowing they were the telepath's only hope—and maybe the Heiren's as well. They didn't acknowledge that out loud, but both cadets were all too aware of it.

Finally, they came to a large, unadorned building the color of new corn, where the façade had been worn away in places to reveal the gray bricks beneath it. The lieutenant and his companion stopped on the near side of a big, wide-open plaza and watched their prey vanish inside.

At least, that was how it looked at first. Then one of the abductors came out again and sat on a barrel beside the door, as if to pass the time of day. In reality, of course, he had been posted as a lookout.

Kirk took in the situation at a glance, then withdrew behind a decorative piece of wall. "It looks like this is where they're going to hole up," he observed.

Mitchell took a look for himself. "I wouldn't be surprised."

"We should go for help," the lieutenant said.

"That was the plan," the underclassman agreed.

But now that they were actually about to execute it,

his expression had changed. He seemed to have his doubts.

"What is it?" asked Kirk.

Mitchell shook his head. "The more I think about it," he said, "the less confidence I have that Ar Bintor's security people are trained to deal with hostage situations."

The lieutenant looked at him. The man was right, of course. "They'll wind up surrounding the place . . ."

"At which point the kidnappers will either bide their time . . ."

"Or kill the telepath," Kirk acknowledged.

"Either way," said Mitchell, "they'll screw up the ceremony."

The lieutenant nodded thoughtfully. "Then it's up to us."

"Once again."

Kirk took a moment to consider their next move. One thing was clear to him—they needed more information.

"I'd say a little reconnaissance is in order," he said.

"I'd say you're right," Mitchell replied.

"You scout around to the left," the lieutenant decided, "and I'll scout to the right. We'll rendezvous back here."

"Got it," said the plebe.

Several minutes later, they returned to the decorative piece of wall. Mitchell didn't look as if he had found anything particularly encouraging. But then, neither had Kirk.

"The only easy way in," the lieutenant observed, "is through the front door—but I think that Heiren sitting on the barrel is going to have something to say about that."

Mitchell grunted. "You think so?"

"On the other hand," said Kirk, ignoring the remark, "I saw some third floor windows on my side of the building. They looked big enough to climb through . . . if there was any way to get to them."

The underclassman looked intrigued. "I found a drainpipe on the other side of the building. There were no windows, and the street there wound up in a dead end. But . . ."

The lieutenant saw what Mitchell was getting at. "If we can get up the drainpipe, then come down on the other side of the roof . . ."

"We can get to the windows you found." The plebe frowned. "But to reach the drainpipe, we'll still have to get past the guard. If he sounds the alarm, the jig'll be up."

"So we're back to square one," said Kirk.

"Looks that way."

The upperclassman swore beneath his breath. There had to be a way to get into that dead-end street.

If there had been a crowd in the square, he mused, they might have made their way through it without being noticed and reached the street that way. However, the plaza was nearly deserted, with only a few pedestrians belatedly making their way to the celebration in the center of town.

Mitchell sighed. "I'm sure if that guard understood the magnitude of our problem, he'd look the other way."

"No doubt," the lieutenant gibed back. "On the

other hand, he might think it rude of us to come calling now. He and his friends have abducted someone of importance. They probably want some time to make their captive comfortable before they start thinking about entertaining visitors."

The underclassman looked at him with feigned surprise. "Was that by any chance a joke?"

Kirk grunted. "Lord help me, I guess it was."

"Looks like I'm beginning to rub off on you."

"Lucky me," said the lieutenant.

The two of them pondered their problem some more. Unfortunately, it didn't seem to get them anywhere.

"You know," Mitchell pointed out, "if we wait too long, even rescuing the telepath won't save the ceremony."

"That occurred to me," said Kirk.

"So we've not only got to get across the square without being seen, we've got to do it quickly."

"Piece of cake," the lieutenant responded sarcastically.

"Sure," said Mitchell. "We're two highly trained Starfleet cadets. There's nothing we can't do if we put our minds to it."

"Nothing," Kirk echoed ironically.

Neither of them said anything for a moment or two.

"So," asked Mitchell, "you have anything in mind yet?"

"Not a thing," the lieutenant replied.

"Me, either."

"But I haven't stopped working on it," Kirk assured him.

Then the upperclassman heard a sound behind them . . . a distant rumbling that echoed from building to building in the narrow street. Turning to find the source of it, he spotted a big, bulky wagon up the hill. It was trundling its way toward them, bouncing along on the cobblestones.

In accordance with Heir'at's strictures against modern technology, the thing was pulled by two beasts of burden—each one a pale, smooth-skinned brute with a triangular head, six heavy legs, and a set of curved horns protruding from its shoulders. The cargo was stored in the back of the wagon under a thick, lashed-down layer of hide.

Suddenly, it hit him. "I've got an idea," Kirk told his companion.

"A way to get to the drainpipe?" Mitchell asked.

"Uh-huh." The lieutenant pointed to the wagon. "And there it is."

Mitchell looked at him. "Are we going to knock out the driver? Or take the time to bribe him with something?"

"Neither," said Kirk. "In fact, if we play our cards right, he'll never know he's the key to our plan."

The plebe looked skeptical. "If you say so."

Of course, there was only a fifty-fifty chance that the lieutenant's scheme would get them access to the drainpipe, considering that the wagon would have to turn one way or the other when it got to the square. But to Kirk's mind, fifty percent was better than nothing.

"Come on," he said. "Our carriage awaits."

Then he led Mitchell up the incline of the street,

staying to the shadows along the buildings' eastern walls. It only took them a couple of minutes to pass the wagon and its unsuspecting driver, who darted a curious look at them as they went by.

"I thought that was our carriage," the plebe whispered.

"It is," the lieutenant confirmed.

Making certain the driver didn't notice, he turned and caught up with the wagon. Then he untied one of the lashings that held its cargo in place and beckoned to Mitchell.

The underclassman didn't hesitate. He followed Kirk, clambered in under the piece of hide, and held it up for the other man to do the same. The lieutenant joined him a moment later. When they were both secure in the back of the wagon, Kirk retied the leather lashing with a slipknot and settled back into the darkness.

For a moment, they sat there in silence, bumping up and down along with the wagon. Then Mitchell uttered a sound of heartfelt revulsion.

"My god!" he rasped. "This is disgusting!"

"Keep your voice down," the lieutenant warned him, fully aware of what the underclassman was complaining about.

"But these bags underneath us. They're full of—"

"Manure," said Kirk. "I know."

"You know?" the plebe asked incredulously.

"I knew before we even got into the wagon," the upperclassman told him.

"And you still thought this was a good idea?"

"I grew up in Iowa, remember? On a working

farm," said Kirk, "you get accustomed to the smell of fertilizer."

"Well, New York City didn't have any working farms. I've got to get out of here before I suffocate."

"You're not going anywhere," the lieutenant told him.

"But I can't—"

Kirk remained steadfast. "That's an order, mister. If I can stand it, you can stand it."

Mitchell sounded as if he was going to retch. But somehow, he managed to keep his gorge down. And with each passing moment, no matter how slowly it seemed to go by, they rumbled closer to their objective.

Finally, the upperclassman felt the wagon slow down. It seemed to him they were going to turn. But which way?

"Left," Kirk whispered, as if he could direct their progress by sheer force of will. "Turn left."

"Relax," Mitchell whispered in return. "We're heading in the direction of the drainpipe."

The lieutenant looked at him, though he couldn't see much in the darkness under the hide. "How do you know that?" he wondered.

"You're still asking?"

Kirk felt like slapping his forehead with the heel of his hand. Mitchell's flashes of insight, he thought— they really did come in handy sometimes.

Sure enough, the wagon leaned to the right and then turned ponderously to the left. Just as Mitchell had predicted, they were heading for the street on the left side of the warehouse. So far, the lieutenant thought, luck had remained their loyal companion.

But they weren't out of the woods yet—not by a long shot. The cadets still had to sneak out the back of the wagon without the kidnappers' lookout noticing them. And then they had to hope that Mitchell's drainpipe could hold up under their weight.

Kirk counted to ten, then untied the slipknot that held their covering in place. Lifting the edge of the hide, he took a peek in what he estimated was the guard's direction. The plebe peeked too.

The lieutenant could see the kidnapper. At the moment, the Heiren was looking the other way, distracted by something. And their wagon was about to pass the dead-end street.

"Get ready," he told his fellow cadet. "Just another couple of seconds more. Okay, let's—"

"No!" Mitchell grated, groping for Kirk's arm.

The lieutenant stopped and looked at him, trying to make him out in the darkness. "What is it?"

"Nature calls," said the underclassman, with uncanny certainty. "Our friend the lookout is going to go into the building and ask someone to take his place for a while."

This time, Kirk didn't ask him how he knew. He just reined in his impatience and waited.

A moment later, he was glad he had listened to Mitchell, because the guard got up and walked into the warehouse. For at least a little while, the door to the building was unwatched.

Amazing, Kirk thought. The plebe's powers of

intuition were even sharper than he had imagined. He wondered *how* sharp.

But for the time being, the lieutenant had more immediate concerns on his mind. He was tempted to follow the sentinel inside and try to subdue him quickly and quietly. Then, if he was successful, he and Mitchell could try to rescue the telepath.

After all, there was a lot to be said for the element of surprise. That was one of the first bits of wisdom Kirk had absorbed in his freshman-year command-tactics class.

Then again, surprise or no surprise, he didn't know what kind of opposition they would be facing inside. Better to follow their original plan, bide their time, and hope for a better window of opportunity.

After all, he told himself, they were only going to get one shot at this. They had to make it a good one.

Slipping out from under the hide covering, Kirk dropped to the ground and slipped into the dead-end street. Mitchell, he saw, was right behind him. With the wagon groaning and jerking under the considerable weight of its cargo, the driver didn't seem to notice their departure any more than he had noticed their arrival.

Satisfied that they hadn't drawn any attention yet, the lieutenant checked out the drainpipe he had spied earlier. Fortunately, it was in good condition. In fact, the pipe looked almost new. It was a good thing, too, considering how critical it was to their plan.

Kirk started to climb first, using the brackets that fastened the pipe to the wall for hand- and footholds.

Looking back over his shoulder, he assured himself that Mitchell was following him up.

The lieutenant was just shy of the roof when he heard his companion swear beneath his breath. Wondering what had happened, Kirk looked down again and saw Mitchell's distress.

"They're coming!" the underclassman whispered.

Spurred by the tone of urgency in Mitchell's voice, the lieutenant clambered that much faster. He made it onto the roof, threw himself flat, and reached over the edge for his companion.

Mitchell didn't take the helping hand. In fact, as far as Kirk could tell, the other man had stopped climbing altogether. Cursing to himself, the upperclassman peered over the edge of the roof to see why—though he had a feeling he already knew.

His fears were substantiated when he saw a pair of Heiren dressed in festive garments down below. They were peering down the dead-end street from the square—looking for something, apparently.

What was worse, Kirk recognized them. They were the tall, burly specimens who had carried the telepath in the carpet there on their shoulders. Judging from the hands they held inside their long, gaily decorated robes, they had weapons concealed in them.

To that point, the kidnappers hadn't seen Mitchell clinging to the drainpipe, just a foot or two beneath the line of the roof. But if they chanced to look up . . .

"Are you sure?" asked one of them.

The other one shrugged. "I thought I was."

"Maybe it was a scavenger."

"Maybe," the second one conceded.

The Heiren craned his neck to look down the dead-end street some more. Then, apparently unable to find anything, he left. The other kidnapper went with him without another word.

As soon as the Heiren were gone, Mitchell heaved a sigh and climbed the rest of the way up. "I was certain they were going to use me for target practice," he said, rolling his way onto the roof.

"We were lucky," Kirk agreed.

The other man shook his head. "Not me. If I was lucky, I would've been on this roof before they got here."

He had a point, the lieutenant admitted—if only to himself. Then he got up and set out across the roof, careful not to make too much noise. A moment later, Mitchell came after him.

The roof peaked in the middle, but not so steeply that the cadets were in any real danger of losing their footing. They negotiated the peak and reached the opposite side without a hint of a mishap. Then they got down on their hands and knees to look down.

The windows Kirk had mentioned were just below them—and as luck would have it, they seemed to be wide open. It wouldn't be difficult for the cadets to lower themselves and swing inside.

On the other hand, they didn't know what kind of situation they were swinging into, or what the odds against them might be. Kirk said as much.

"Doesn't appear we've got much choice," Mitchell responded.

"Just be ready," the lieutenant advised him. "For anything."

Then he took the lead, turning around and grabbing the edge of the roof with his fingers. With a last look at his companion, he jumped down and swung himself through the window aperture.

Chapter Sixteen

KIRK'S LANDING inside the building was flawless. His feet were spread at shoulder width, his weight evenly distributed. Had any of the telepath's abductors been inside, he would have been as ready for them as an unarmed human could possibly be.

As it was, he found himself in an empty room, devoid of any immediate threat to life and limb. In fact, the only company he had was a few wooden boxes and a floor full of dust. That changed a moment later, as Mitchell swung in after him.

The underclassman looked around quickly, then came to the same conclusion Kirk had. Turning to the lieutenant, Mitchell whispered, "No welcome wagon? I'm disappointed."

Kirk didn't dignify the remark with a response. Instead, he pointed to the room's only door.

Together, he and Mitchell approached it and listened. They could hear voices, some louder than others. Every so often, one of the dissidents beyond the door laughed. *And why not?* the lieutenant thought. *They had accomplished their mission.*

Now it was up to the cadets to do the same.

Slowly, quietly, Kirk took the handle of the door and pulled it inward. Not much—just a crack, really, so as not to draw any attention. Then he snuck a peek into the hallway outside.

He saw two Heiren lounging on a landing, not far from a flight of stairs. They were exchanging ribald jokes and passing a dark leather drinking skin back and forth, their yellow eyes slitted with glee in their blunt, bronze faces. To that point, the kidnappers seemed unaware that anyone had invaded their stronghold.

Pulling his head back, Kirk turned to Mitchell. He held up two fingers, signifying what they were up against. The other man smiled and massaged his knuckles meaningfully.

The lieutenant scowled at him. This wasn't a training exercise, for pity's sake. This was the real thing, with real adversaries out for real blood. If the two of them didn't get the job done, entire planets' worth of people would pay the price.

Yet Mitchell seemed unimpressed. To him, it appeared, this was just another another romp. In fact, *everything* was just another romp.

The plebe's smile widened, as if he knew exactly what Kirk was thinking. "Lead on," he whispered.

The lieutenant peered through the opening again. The two kidnappers still hadn't noticed that anything was awry. If anything, they were more engrossed in their storytelling than they had been before.

This had to be quick, Kirk told himself. It had to be over before the Heiren knew what had hit them, or their comrades would come running upstairs to lend a hand.

He took a breath. Then he flung the door open, took a couple of running steps, and launched himself through the air. He came down on top of one of the Heiren, who didn't even have a chance to cry for assistance before the lieutenant clamped a hand over his scaly mouth.

Together, cadet and kidnapper hit the rail and slipped to the floor. Fortunately, Kirk landed on top of his opponent, a situation that enabled him to use his weight to good advantage.

Out of the corner of his eye, the lieutenant saw Mitchell tackle the other kidnapper, but he didn't have the luxury of waiting to see how their fight came out. He was too busy taking part in his own.

The Heiren Kirk faced was strong, like most of his species, but the lieutenant was quicker. Keeping his left hand clamped tightly over the kidnapper's mouth, he warded off a blow from a heavy bronze fist with his right. Then he pulled back and drove the heel of his hand into the bridge of the Heiren's nose.

It stunned the dissident, leaving him defenseless. Kirk's second blow knocked the Heiren unconscious altogether.

Springing to his feet, the lieutenant got ready to

assist Mitchell. But it seemed the underclassman had the situation well in hand. His target was laid out flat on the floor, his eyes closed and a trickle of green blood running from each nostril.

"Good work," Kirk breathed.

"Tell me about it," came the less-than-modest reply. "So what do we do now?" Mitchell asked.

The lieutenant didn't know where the telepath was being held, or how many of the kidnappers and their comrades were present in the warehouse. But if he and Mitchell had to conduct their search in their uniforms, he didn't think they would get very far.

Then he glanced at the unconscious Heiren, with their long, loose-fitting robes and their generous hoods. With such clothing to conceal their appearances, Kirk and his companion might make their way through the building without fear of being discovered. That is, if their enemies didn't look at them too closely.

"So?" the plebe prodded.

In response to Mitchell's question, the upperclassman pointed to the two unconscious kidnappers. Then he jerked a thumb in the direction of the room they'd just come from.

"Quickly," he added.

The plebe looked at him for a moment. Then understanding dawned and he smiled.

Without any further ado, they dragged their victims into the room with the dust and the boxes. Pulling off the Heiren's robes and hoods, the cadets them on over their uniforms.

"Spiffy," said Mitchell, patting down his new garb. "Of course, they could fit a little better. . . ."

"We'll get you a tailor later," the lieutenant replied. "After we get the telepath out of here."

Suddenly, the plebe's expression changed. He plumbed the bottom of a pocket he had found in his robe. Then he took something out and held it where Kirk could see it.

It was small and strangely shaped, but there was no question as to its function. The device was a directed-energy weapon—the sort of technology that was forbidden in Heir'at.

"Obviously," said Mitchell, tilting his head in the direction of his victim, "my friend the kidnapper doesn't have the same regard for tradition that we do."

The lieutenant searched his own pockets—and found the same kind of device in one of them. "I'd say he's not the only one," he observed, inspecting the thing as he turned it over in his hand.

It put an entirely different spin on the situation. The cadets were a good deal more dangerous with directed-energy weapons at their disposal. But then, so were the dissidents.

And there were a lot more of them.

Kirk set his device on stun. It was Starfleet policy. Reluctantly, Mitchell did the same.

"Come on," said the lieutenant.

"Right with you," said his companion.

And they began their search for the telepath.

* * *

Mitchell followed Kirk down the stairs. His hand was stuffed into his robe pocket so he could keep his weapon concealed, but his heart was pumping so hard it seemed impossible the kidnappers wouldn't hear it.

Somewhere down below, on one of the warehouse's lower floors, the cadets would soon be risking their lives to rescue a being they had never met, from what might turn out to be an army of alien fanatics.

They might fail. Worse, they might die. But Mitchell couldn't bring himself to ponder any of that. All he could think about at the moment was how much fun he was having.

He had joined Starfleet to touch the stars, to go where no man had gone before. But this trail of intrigue and adventure . . . this leaping from rooftops and scaling walls . . . it stirred him as he had never imagined anything could, all the way to the depths of his soul.

As for Kirk . . . who knew? The man still seemed as freezer-unit serious as ever. But he was also starting to take some serious chances . . . and just a little while ago, he had actually attempted a joke. Mitchell was finding it easier and easier to hold out hope for him.

Not that they would ever become friends again— not after the lieutenant's determined announcement to the contrary. But if the plebe could make Kirk loosen up some more, if he could unearth a person from that stack of textbook tapes, that would be satisfaction enough.

Suddenly, the lieutenant held his hand up—a signal that he had seen something or someone down

Michael Jan Friedman

below. Peering past the handrail, Mitchell saw an open door—and a flash of colorful robes beyond it.

There was conversation—not the jesting of the two whose clothes they had taken, but something of a more sober nature. As Mitchell tried to listen in, he could hear another voice.

But he didn't hear it with his ears, as he had heard the others. This voice was in his head.

It didn't speak in words, either. It spoke in sentiments, attitudes, emotions. Or maybe it just seemed that way, he thought, because that was all he could understand of it.

Still, one thing seemed absolutely certain to him, so certain he would have bet his life on it. The telepath they had come to rescue was in the room with the open door.

Excited about the discovery, the underclassman tapped Kirk on the shoulder. After all, now that the telepath had contacted them, they had to agree on a way to get the poor guy out of there.

But when the lieutenant turned around in response, his expression wasn't anything like what Mitchell had expected. Kirk seemed surprised, expectant—as if he were waiting for the underclassman to give him some urgent new piece of tactical data.

As if he hadn't heard the telepath's summons at all.

Mitchell pointed to his temple. But Kirk shook his head, a crease forming at the bridge of his nose. Obviously, he didn't have the slightest idea what Mitchell was referring to.

Interesting, the plebe thought. *Whatever the telepath is transmitting, I'm the only one receiving it.*

He had always suspected that his flashes of insight were just the tip of the iceberg . . . that his brain was somehow more sensitive to telepathic stimuli than the average human's. Here, it seemed, was some evidence to back the up.

Unfortunately, the underclassman would have to explore the question another time. At that moment, his first concern had to be his mission.

Kirk shrugged, no doubt wondering why Mitchell had tapped him. The plebe frowned and directed his companion to the open door. Then he mouthed the words "He's in there. The te-le-path."

The lieutenant turned and regarded his fellow cadet. For a second or two, he seemed to ponder how Mitchell might know such a thing. Finally, he just appeared to accept it.

"What do we do?" asked the underclassman, his voice barely a whisper. After all, the telepath hadn't given him any instructions.

The lieutenant frowned, peered past the handrail at what else he could see of the building's second floor, and finally turned back to his colleague. "We go in blasting," he mouthed back.

And that's what they did.

The cadets walked down the rest of the stairs, careful to keep their weapons in their pockets—so if any of the other dissidents caught sight of them, they wouldn't suspect anything was wrong. Then they entered the room as casually as they could—and used the fraction of a second their disguises bought them to assess the situation.

Mitchell saw five figures.

Four were standing, their heads turning to see who had come in. All of them had weapons in their hands identical to the ones the cadets had "borrowed," though they held the devices cavalierly, almost carelessly. Clearly, they weren't expecting to have to use them anytime soon.

The fifth figure was seated, his arms and legs bound to a chair with leather thongs. He was a tall, lean Heiren of middle age, wearing a simple white robe with dark blue trim, and he didn't appear the least bit surprised by the humans' appearance. In fact, it seemed to Mitchell that he had been waiting for them.

One of the kidnappers began to speak—perhaps to challenge the newcomers' presence there. But before he could get his question out, Kirk drew his weapon and blasted the Heiren with a stream of dark blue energy. At the same time, Mitchell took out one of the kidnapper's comrades.

Before the unconscious bodies of their adversaries could skid into the wall behind them, the cadets took aim at the two remaining dissidents in the room. Unfortunately, the Heiren had raised their weapons by then and were taking aim as well.

Four sapphire-colored beams sliced through the air. Two missed, though one of them came close enough to Mitchell's ribs to burn a hole in his robes. The other two beams found their targets, knocking the kidnappers senseless.

It all took place in the space of a second. By the time the plebe's heart started beating again, it was over.

The combat had taken place quickly and quietly, with a minimum of trouble, exactly the way he and Kirk had hoped it would. And as the cadets had also hoped, they had won.

The bronze-skinned figure in the chair looked up at them—first at Kirk, then at Mitchell—as they put their weapons away. His yellow eyes remained locked with the underclassman's.

"You're the sensitive," he said.

"I guess so," Mitchell responded. The Heiren's remark seemed to confirm his suspicions about his abilities.

The telepath's eyes narrowed into slits. "You're a rarity," he observed. "Just as I am."

"If you say so," said the underclassman.

Kirk looked from one of them to the other. Then he went over to the telepath and began to tug on the prisoner's bonds.

"Now that we've gotten to know each other," he declared, "maybe we can think about getting out of here."

"Let's go back the way we came in," Mitchell suggested.

It seemed like the most obvious route. After all, they weren't likely to meet with any resistance, and going down the drainpipe would be easier than going up.

"Sounds good to me," said Kirk.

But before they could go anywhere, they heard a loud voice that seemed to climb the stairs. It was calling a name.

The cadets looked at each other. As the lieutenant

worked harder to free the telepath, Mitchell moved to the door and closed it.

Again, the voice called, only slightly muffled by the door. There was no response. What's more, the underclassman thought he knew why.

"They're on to us," he concluded, taking out his weapon again. "Our friends upstairs must have been due to check in or something."

"Could be," Kirk replied.

With a determined tug, he pulled away the last of the ropes that bound the telepath's wrists. Then he knelt to attack the bonds that restricted the Heiren's ankles.

Suddenly, they heard a rush of feet up the stairs. For a moment, Mitchell thought the door to their room would be flung open—but it wasn't. Instead, the commotion seemed to pass them by.

"We can't get out that way anymore," Mitchell observed, doing his best to remain calm.

But it wasn't easy. Cold sweat was trickling between the underclassman's shoulder blades, and his heart was beating so hard he thought his ribs were going to splinter.

Suddenly, it occurred to him, their gambit didn't seem like quite so much fun anymore.

"We'll have to go out the front door," Kirk responded.

"That'll be guarded too," Mitchell reminded him.

The lieutenant clenched his jaw and whipped away the last of the Heiren's bonds. "Beggars can't be choosers."

Oh, good, thought the plebe, as the telepath stood

up on uncertain legs. *Just what we need in our moment of jeopardy—platitudes from the ol' professor.*

But Kirk seemed to have more than platitudes in mind. He pulled the big, colorful robe away from one of the Heiren they had stunned and held it out for the telepath.

"Put it on," he said.

The telepath did as he was told. Last of all, he pulled the robe's hood up over his head.

"Now follow my lead," the lieutenant told them.

Then he took out his weapon, opened the door, and looked both ways. Satisfied that the way was clear, he headed for the stairs. Mitchell and the telepath had little choice but to fall in behind him.

As they began their descent, the underclassman caught a glimpse of what awaited them. The first floor of the warehouse was one big room, designed to store anything that could fit through the front door. But at the moment, it held only dissidents.

There had to be ten or twelve of them, at least—it was difficult to tell at a glance. But clearly, the cadets were outnumbered. They wouldn't stand a chance in a firefight.

And even with their hoods pulled up, they weren't going to fool the kidnappers for more than a couple of seconds. One of their enemies was bound to see through their disguises and blow the whistle on them.

Kirk had to have come to much the same conclusion. Still, the lieutenant continued to make his way down the stairs undaunted, as if the warehouse and everything in it belonged to him.

Suddenly, without warning, Kirk whirled and

aimed his energy weapon at Mitchell's face. At least, that was how it seemed to the cadet. It took him a fraction of a second to realize Kirk was aiming past him, at something up the stairs. He spun around to see what it was.

But there was nothing there.

As Mitchell tried to figure out what was going on, the lieutenant pressed his trigger. His weapon spat a stream of dark blue fire, punching a hole in the second-floor ceiling.

"They're trying to escape!" he bellowed—loudly enough to be heard back in the bakery, all the way across town.

Then he fired a second time, smashing a second hole in the ceiling next to the first.

That got the attention of the Heiren gathered on the first floor. Whipping out their directed-energy devices, they assaulted the stairs, ascending them two steps at a time. With their festive robes, they looked like a multicolored river that had decided to defy gravity by flowing upstream.

Mitchell watched the Heiren flow around him as if he were a rock in a raging current, Kirk on one side of him and the telepath on the other. Before he knew it, the dissidents had left them behind—and the way to the front door was as clear as it could be.

The plebe took a moment—and only a moment—to appreciate what the lieutenant had accomplished, and to ask himself why *he* hadn't thought of it. Then he grabbed the telepath by the arm and escorted him the rest of the way down the stairs.

Chapter Seventeen

JIM KIRK was giddy with success.

He had hoodwinked a whole roomful of alien kidnappers. And not only that, he had done it on the spur of the moment, without any of the careful, deliberate planning on which he normally prided himself.

It was a lesson. No—more than that. It was a revelation. There was a lot to be said for acting impulsively—for following your instincts when the odds were against you.

The proof of it was right across the room from him. The warehouse's front door stood unguarded and uncontested, abandoned by the kidnappers in their rush to follow Kirk's ruse.

Smiling despite himself, the lieutenant approached the door and reached for its handle. But before he could turn it, he heard a voice roll like thunder behind him.

"Stop them! They've got the telepath!"

It was almost the same thing he himself had shouted moments earlier. But this time, it was the truth.

Whirling, Kirk identified the source of the warning—a tall, broad-shouldered Heiren with an ugly scar across the bridge of his nose and an energy weapon pointed menacingly in their direction. Without hesitating, the lieutenant raised his own weapon. Mitchell, who was standing right beside him, did the same.

All three of them fired at the same time. It wasn't clear whether the cadets both hit their target, or if it was only one of them. All that was certain was that the Heiren missed, and that he went flying backward into the wall a moment later.

The lieutenant didn't wait to see the kidnapper tumble down the stairs. He didn't wait to see if the Heiren's cry turned his comrades around and brought them clamoring in pursuit. He just turned the handle on the door, flung it open, and cleared the steps ahead of him with a leap.

But even before he landed on the cobblestones outside, he saw that he and his comrades weren't out of the woods yet. Instead of the single sentinel who had been sitting on the barrel outside the warehouse, Kirk saw a handful of Heiren clustered on either side of the steps.

There were six or seven of them in all—and the

lieutenant didn't believe for a minute it was just a social gathering. Something had aroused the kidnappers' suspicions and encouraged them to send out more guards.

Of course, if there were any trouble, they had expected it to come from the square outside—not from the warehouse itself. So as Kirk emerged, the sentinels were too surprised to react right away. They hesitated for a fraction of a second, and it proved their undoing.

Rolling as he landed, the lieutenant came up in a kneeling position and fired. As closely as the Heiren were clustered, it was hardly a surprise that he hit one of them.

As Kirk felled a second dissident, Mitchell and the telepath emerged from the building as well. But they didn't look shocked at all at the size of the gathering. It was as if they had anticipated it.

By then, a couple of the Heiren had drawn their weapons and were returning the human's fire. The others, realizing what was happening, went after the underclassman and the telepath.

Unfortunately, Kirk couldn't help his companions grapple with the enemy. The best strategy for him at the moment was to take out as many of the dissidents as he could.

He aimed and fired a third time.

For what could only have been a few seconds, chaos reigned in the square. The few innocents present ran away screaming, fearing for their lives. Dark blue beams lanced this way and that, spattering off wall after ancient wall and slamming into body after robed body. Somehow, the lieutenant avoided being one of the bodies that were hit.

Then, as if by magic, there were no other targets left for him to fire at, and no one left to return his fire. All but two of his adversaries were stretched out on the ground.

Mitchell was exhanging jabs with one of the two who were still standing. The other was wrestling with the telepath, the pair of them too close for Kirk to draw a bead on the kidnapper.

Cursing beneath his breath, he put his weapon away and started to go to the telepath's aid. But before the lieutenant could get near the fracas, one of the two most important beings on Heir'tza reared back and planted his heel in his enemy's midsection.

The dissident doubled over, and the telepath chopped down on the back of his neck. A moment later, the kidnapper collapsed in a heap.

At the same time, Mitchell landed a combination of his own—a right to the jaw and a left to the side of the head. When his adversary crumpled, having been knocked senseless, the cadet looked around for another one.

But, of course, there weren't any kidnappers left. Together, Kirk and his allies had polished them all off.

The upperclassman had a strange inclination to applaud the work they had done. As it was, he found himself exchanging a look with his fellow cadet—an expression of pride, a recognition of all the two of them had accomplished to that point.

Words couldn't have expressed the sentiment any better. At least, that was how it seemed to Kirk.

Then the moment was over and the lieutenant turned to the telepath, who was massaging a set of knuckles he had scraped in the melee. "They didn't tell us you could fight like that," he told the Heiren.

The telepath smiled, exposing long, white fangs. "I don't often get the chance," he noted.

Suddenly, they heard voices from inside the warehouse. *Angry* voices—and a thunder of footfalls on the winding stairs.

"Come on," said Kirk, waving the telepath past him as he pulled out his weapon again. "We'd better get out of here."

After all, they had a ceremony to get to. And after all they had gone through, it would be a pity if they were late.

As it happened, Mitchell and his friends crossed the plaza and lost themselves in the streets of Heir'at before the rest of the kidnappers could catch up with them.

"We made it," said the plebe, casting a look over his shoulder down a long, winding street.

"Not yet, we haven't," Kirk responded. "We've still got a long way to go before we reach the temple." He turned to the telepath. "By the way, which one are we headed for?"

"The Eastern Temple," the Heiren told him. "The closer one, as luck would have it."

"The Eastern Temple it is, then," said the lieutenant. "Just stick with me and keep your eyes open."

Michael Jan Friedman

"I will endeavor to do both," the telepath assured him.

As Kirk led the way, ever vigilant, Mitchell came up alongside the Heiren. "So . . . do you have a name?" he asked.

His yellow eyes narrowing with amusement, the telepath nodded. "I do indeed. My name is Perris. Perris Nodarh."

"Pleased to meet you, Perris Nodarh. I'm Gary Mitchell. And our friend the pathfinder up there is Jim Kirk."

"Names I will have to remember," the Heiren told him. "In fact, every Heir'och and Heir'tza will be obliged to remember them, if all goes well the remainder of this day."

The thought appealed to Mitchell. It appealed to him a lot.

Being a hero, having alien schoolchildren honor his name . . . none of those perks had even occurred to him when he took the test to enter the Academy. And he had just gotten started.

"They told us which telepath would come from the Eastern Temple," he told the Heiren, "but, frankly, I don't recall what they said."

"And you wish to know which faction I represent?" The telepath seemed amused by the cadet's honesty.

Mitchell nodded sheepishly. "I suppose that's what I was asking, in my clumsy way."

"I am Heir'och," said Perris Nodarh.

"So your kidnappers were Heir'tza?"

"No." The telepath shook his scaly head. "They were Heir'och as well, judging from what I could pick

218

up of their conversation. They seized me because they oppose the Reconciliation."

"Takes all kinds," said Mitchell.

"Yes," said the Heiren. "Though I look forward to the day when all my people will be *one* kind."

It was slow, careful going for a while after that. Kirk forced them to skulk through narrow alleyways and slip from cover to cover, working their way toward the center of town at a pace that a Central Park box turtle would have been ashamed of.

Mitchell found himself growing more and more impatient. He had an urge to speed things up, to make a beeline for the temple where the telepath was supposed to appear and the devil take the hindmost.

But he curbed the impulse and kept his mouth shut—because like it or not, he knew the lieutenant's approach was the right one. If they picked up the pace and ran into one of their enemies, all their good work might be undone in an instant.

And none of them wanted that.

So they kept to their indirect route until the streets they traveled became more crowded with Heir'tza and Heir'och, and they were able to blend with the general flow of celebrants. But even then, they moved more slowly than they would have liked, the city's byways choked with unusually heavy traffic.

Eventually, they emerged from a broad thoroughfare and caught sight of the Eastern Temple. Rising from a glittering sea of Heiren, the temple turned out to be an ornate, five-story building with a splendid, golden roof and a slender stone tower rising from each corner.

"We're almost there," Mitchell noted.

The telepath nodded. "Thanks to you and your colleague."

Kirk didn't say anything. He was too busy looking around for anything suspicious. But then, thought the plebe, he wouldn't have expected any less from the man.

The last few hundred meters were the toughest, as they wove their way through the densest part of the throng to the pall of the temple. And still they saw no sign of the telepath's abductors.

To Mitchell's mind, there was nothing especially odd about that. They had gotten a head start, after all. With the crowd in their way, the kidnappers simply hadn't managed to close the gap.

Finally, they reached the pitted, stone steps of the temple. Though the building was open to anyone who wished to enter and pray, as ancient custom demanded, the only ones occupying the steps at the moment were a half-dozen security personnel in red-and-white uniforms.

Kirk broke through the first rank of onlookers, opening the way for Mitchell and the telepath. Then, with a last wary glance at the crowd, he led them in the direction of the temple entrance.

The entire way there, no one around them had been inclined to look under their hoods, so no one had noticed that the cadets weren't Heiren. Apparently, the guards around the temple were a good deal more discerning. Within seconds, a pair of high-ranking officers had converged on Mitchell and his companions.

"You're offworlders," one of them noted bluntly, his eyes narrowing beneath his jutting brow ridge.

"We're Starfleet," Kirk said.

The guards looked skeptical, to say the least. "What are you doing here?" asked the second one.

"We were assigned to protect the Heir'och telepath," the underclassman told them. He jerked a thumb over his shoulder. "That's him."

The Heiren looked past him at Perris Nodarh. The telepath removed his hood so they could see his face.

"The Heir'och telepath," the first guard echoed. He didn't sound any less skeptical than before.

"It's true," said Perris Nodarh.

"So you say," remarked the second guard, his eyes becoming slits. "But for all we know, you could be a Heir'och terrorist in a white robe."

"We came from the bakery," Kirk pointed out hopefully.

The Heiren shrugged. "That means nothing to us."

"That's where the telepath was hidden," the lieutenant insisted.

"Or so you say," came the response.

Mitchell sighed. He had expected this to be the easy part.

"Can't you contact Minister Bintor?" he asked. "He would clear this up in a matter of—"

He stopped himself. With advanced technology restricted in Heir'at, Ar Bintor might as well have been at the other end of the galaxy. They couldn't contact him any more than they could contact Earth.

The underclassman decided to change tacks. "Surely," he said, "there's someone inside the temple who knows what the telepath looks like? The person in charge of things, maybe?"

The first Heir'tza turned to him. "You would *like* to get inside the temple, wouldn't you?"

Kirk shook his head, obviously as baffled as the plebe was. "If you didn't know what the telepath looked like or where he was coming from, how were you supposed to know when he arrived?"

The guards glanced at each other, as if trying to decide how much to divulge. Finally, the second one spoke.

"He was to be escorted here by Tev Nallor, Minister Bintor's second-in-command. But, unless my eyesight has begun to desert me, Tev Nallor is nowhere to be seen."

"He's probably back at the bakery," Mitchell declared, "trying to figure out what happened to the telepath he was supposed to guard." Something occurred to him for the first time. "Unless . . ."

"What?" asked the first guard.

"Unless he was killed," Mitchell finished.

The security officers' brows ridged over. "Killed?" echoed the first one, his voice taut with concern.

"Yes," said the lieutenant. "There were kidnappers. They seized the telepath. We rescued him."

The second officer snorted derisively. But he couldn't hide his nervousness—at least, not from Mitchell.

The plebe bit his lip. After all they had done, all they had risked, he couldn't believe they were being waylaid on the temple steps, just a few meters shy of their destination.

What's more, he didn't like the idea of standing out in the open, unprotected from directed-energy fire. After all, the telepath's kidnappers had already demonstrated their willingness to use such weapons—and they were probably edging closer to the temple at that very moment.

"Look," he told the guards, "there's got to be some way to prove this man is who he says he is."

The first security officer smiled grimly. "He could read my mind. That would prove it."

The telepath shook his head. "I can't make contact with an ordinary mind. I can only speak with another telepath."

Suddenly, Mitchell got an idea.

"Then speak with me," he said.

Kirk looked at him. You? But you're—"

"A sensitive," the underclassman reminded him. "At least, that's how our friend here described it."

The lieutenant nodded. "Of course."

"What are you going on about?" asked the second guard.

Mitchell turned to him. "One of you tell me something no one else could possibly know. Then I'll turn around so my face is hidden, and the telepath will tell you exactly what you said."

"In other words," said Kirk, in an attempt to clarify the proposition for the security officers, "he'll use his power of telepathy to pluck the thought from your head?"

"Exactly," Mitchell confirmed.

The upperclassman turned to Perris Nodarh. "Are you certain you can pull this off?"

"I believe so," said the telepath.

He didn't sound entirely sure. But then, how could he be? There were no other full-fledged telepaths on Heir'och—and his attempts to communicate with the plebe had been limited to that one incident in the warehouse.

Still, it was worth a try.

"Well?" Mitchell asked the guards.

The Heiren thought about it. They looked wary.

"It could be a trick," said the second one.

"Time's wasting," Kirk pointed out. "And if this *is* the Heir'och telepath, do you want to be known as the pair who kept the great reconciliation from taking place?" He pointed to the crowd. "Do you want to have to explain yourselves to *them?*"

Judging by the guards' expressions, that put the matter in a different light. The first one made a gesture of surrender.

"Let's see what they can do," he said.

The second one nodded in agreement. "Indeed."

"Excellent," Mitchell responded. He put his hand on the first guard's shoulder as if they were old friends. Then he offered the Heiren his ear. "Go ahead. I'm listening."

The officer thought for a moment. Then he whispered, "My garden was trampled by the crowds."

The plebe nodded, then turned his back to the telepath. "All right," he said. "What am I thinking, Perris?"

He concentrated on the guard's complaint as hard as he could, to the exclusion of all other thoughts. *My garden was trampled by the crowds,* he mused. *My garden was trampled by the crowds. . . .*

For what seemed like a long time, there was no response. There was only the hum and crackle of the assembled onlookers, who must have been wondering feverishly what was going on.

Come on, Mitchell silently encouraged the telepath. *You can do it. Just concentrate, okay? My garden was trampled by the crowds. My garden was trampled by the crowds. . . .*

Abruptly, Perris Nodarh spoke up.

"I'm sorry to hear it," he said sympathetically. "But then, such losses can be remedied. When the celebration is over, I would be glad to help you plant a new one."

Mitchell turned and saw the look on the security officer's face. The Heiren's yellow eyes were wide with amazement beneath his brow ridge, his skepticism gone without a trace.

"That was it," he muttered.

"What was it?" asked the other guard.

"Never mind," said the first one. "We've got to get these three into the temple. Quickly."

Mitchell couldn't have agreed more.

Chapter Eighteen

THANK YOU ONCE AGAIN," said Shirod Lenna, Heir'at's First Minister of Security. "Your intervention in this matter appears to have been most timely, Lieutenant Kirk."

The cadet nodded. "Thank you, sir."

Their voices echoed in the Eastern Temple's primary chamber, a huge room with lofty, vaulted ceilings full of small, flying creatures that resembled hummingbirds. Great events in Heiren history were depicted in glorious murals that covered the entirety of each wall.

The tall, slender windows in the place were made of leaded glass that transformed sunlight into long shafts of various hues. They illuminated a raised, central platform of pink marble, as well as the several ranks of wooden benches arranged in expanding circles around it.

At the moment, the platform was occupied by the barefoot Perris Nodarh and a handful of humble attendants, who were dressing the telepath in a new white robe with blue trim. It was fortunate that the temple staff had had a supply of such garments on hand.

After all, Perris's old robe had been soiled and torn in the fight at the warehouse, then rumpled in the course of his journey across Heir'at. It wouldn't have been appropriate for him to wear it during such a grand occasion as the Reconciliation.

Kirk, on the other hand, was still wearing the robe he had "borrowed" from the telepath's kidnappers. True, it was a little the worse for wear . . . but in the press of the crowd, no one was likely to notice.

"What took place at the bakery is most unsettling," Lenna continued. "Ar Bintor is a close friend of mine. And one of my wife's nieces was serving as a guard there."

The lieutenant bit his lip. He didn't know what to say to that.

Not that he had never experienced a tragedy of his own. As an innocent teenager, he had witnessed the massacre of some four thousand colonists on Tarsus IV—the event that had earned the colony's governor the infamous name Kodos the Executioner.

But even then, he hadn't lost anyone really close to him. His friends and relatives had remained unscathed on Tarsus IV and elsewhere. With luck, he thought, he would be able to say that for a long time to come.

"I didn't see Ar Bintor before we left the bakery," Kirk said at last, offering some hope. "It may be he wasn't hurt after all."

The minister, a tall Heiren with a narrow, bony face, grunted softly. "I hope you're right about that, Lieutenant. Just as I hope some of the kidnappers decided to linger about that warehouse, so we can catch them and try them for their crimes."

Kirk doubted it. Still, he kept his mouth shut. It wasn't his place to tell a Heir'tza security minister about the likelihood of catching dissidents in his own city.

His ears lying flat against his hairless, bronze skull, Lenna shook his head. "Fortunately or unfortunately, we Heiren live in a time of momentous change . . . and change tends to take its toll on all of us."

"Tev Badris says he's ready," came an eager voice. It echoed wildly, almost irreverently, in the temple's cavernous interior.

Kirk turned to the entrance and saw Mitchell. The plebe held his arms up, his colorful reveler's robe rustling like an old friend.

"Well?" he said. "Time and tide and all that."

The telepath couldn't have been familiar with the quote, but he obviously understood the sense of it. "I am ready, my friend," he told Mitchell, his voice echoing as well.

"Great," replied the underclassman, pulling up his hood. He turned to the lieutenant. "We should get going."

"Yes," said Kirk. "We should."

"You're certain you wish to help?" asked Lenna.

The minister had asked the cadets to take up positions along the ceremonial route. Of course, he had fifty security officers planted in the crowd already, which should have been enough. But after the attack on the bakery, Lenna hoped to err on the side of caution.

"Very certain," Kirk assured him. "I mean, we've come this far. We'd like to see our mission through to its conclusion."

"Laudable," said the minister. "I will commend your helpfulness to your commanding officer."

The lieutenant swallowed. He had been trying not to think too much about Captain Bannock's reaction to all of this. After all, the man had gone out of his way to emphasize that the cadets weren't to leave the bakery.

Under *any* circumstances.

Of course, if Kirk and Mitchell had obeyed orders, Perris Nodarh would still have been in the hands of his kidnappers and the Heiren's prospects for reconciliation would have been obliterated. But to Bannock, that wouldn't be the point.

Regardless of the results, the cadets had disobeyed a direct order from their commanding officer. Neither the captain nor anyone else in Starfleet would look favorably on that.

"Of course," Lenna went on, "I should also inform your captain about your use of energy weapons in Heir'at. But under the circumstances, I believe I can forget that detail."

"That's up to you, sir," said Kirk. "I'm obliged to include it in my report either way."

The Heir'tza looked at him with a smile pulling at the corners of his wide mouth. "You are a very dutiful young man, Lieutenant Kirk. Dutiful, perhaps, to a fault."

Kirk smiled ruefully. "It's the only way I know how to be, First Minister. But thank you all the same."

Mitchell raised his arms again in a gesture of impatience. The lieutenant jerked his thumb over his shoulder to remind Lenna of the plebe's presence at the entrance.

"We'll be late," Kirk said.

"By all means, go," the minister responded. "And may fortune smile on you, Lieutenant Kirk."

"On all of us, sir," the lieutenant replied. Then he pulled up his festive hood and joined his colleague.

"I regret you cannot walk alongside me," Perris Nodarh called to Kirk as the human walked by the temple's central platform. "You have done such a good job escorting me to this point, it seems like a shame to say goodbye to you and Cadet Mitchell now."

"We'll still be watching out for you," the lieutenant promised the telepath. "Just in a different way."

Perris smiled. "Then I'm reassured."

Kirk smiled back at the Heiren. Then he crossed the floor of the chamber and led Mitchell out into the street.

* * *

It took Mitchell and his fellow cadet more than twenty minutes to reach a point along the ceremonial route halfway between the Eastern Temple and the Government House. And even then, they were several rows of onlookers away from the action.

But the plebe didn't mind the poor vantage point or the press of Heiren bodies. He didn't even mind the tall ceremonial hat on the heavyset female in front of him.

After all, the sun was high in the sky. The banners hanging from Heir'at's windows were colorful and optimistic. And, from a more practical standpoint, Lenna's red-and-white-uniformed guards appeared to be everywhere along Perris Nodarh's path.

"Well," said Mitchell, "this is it."

"I guess so," said Kirk, scanning the crowd.

"It's all over but the shouting."

"Looks that way," the lieutenant muttered—though his tone said he didn't believe it for a minute.

"You see a problem?" asked Mitchell.

"Not yet," Kirk replied.

"But you expect one?"

The lieutenant shrugged. "It's a possibility."

"The sun could explode. That's a possibility too."

"It certainly is," the upperclassman conceded.

The plebe sighed. "Don't you ever relax?"

"Sure," said Kirk, looking everywhere but at his companion. "When my mission is over."

Mitchell looked at him, amazed. "But right after that, there's another mission. And another one. It never stops."

The lieutenant smiled an ironic smile. "Isn't that the whole point of being in Starfleet?"

"Always being on your toes?" Mitchell asked.

"Always being challenged."

The underclassman pondered the question, as well as the man who had posed it. "For some people, I guess it is."

"And for others?" Kirk inquired—still vigilant, still inspecting everything and everyone.

Mitchell shrugged. "There's time to sit back and consider what you've done. Especially when you've done it as well as we have."

The lieutenant didn't answer him. But it wasn't because he was at a loss for words—the plebe was pretty certain of that. It was because the man didn't want to be distracted.

The underclassman looked out over the sea of Heiren that surrounded them. Sure, he conceded, it was possible Perris Nodarh's kidnappers were somewhere in the crowd, hoping to finish the job they started. But Minister Lenna had planted so many guards among the onlookers, it didn't seem likely there would be any danger.

Even as Mitchell thought that, a cheer erupted from the Heiren positioned closest to the temple steps. Obviously, the telepath had chosen that moment to make his appearance.

"Here he comes," he told Kirk, feeling a thrill of anticipation.

The lieutenant grunted.

"The Heir'och telepath is beginning his historic journey."

Another grunt.

"In a few minutes," Mitchell noted, "Perris will reach the Government House. Then he and the Heir'tza telepath will shake hands and exchange pleasantries, and we can all go home happy."

This time, the plebe got a dirty look. "Are you trying to disturb my concentration on purpose?"

Mitchell smiled to himself. "Who, me?"

"You know," Kirk reminded him, "I could order you to shut up."

The plebe sighed. "Listen to you," he said. "You haven't learned a thing, have you?"

"Learned?" the lieutenant echoed.

"That's right," Mitchell told him. "You need to ease up if you're ever going to—"

Suddenly, something caught the cadet's eye.

A face.

A face he recognized.

Grabbing Kirk's shoulder, he jerked his head in the face's direction. "Look over there," he grated.

The lieutenant followed the gesture. A moment later, his eyes narrowed. "Isn't that—?"

"One of Perris's abductors," Mitchell finished for him. "The man with the scar across his face."

The last time they had seen the man, he was getting thrown into the wall behind him, propelled by the force of a dark blue energy beam. Apparently, the Heiren had made a complete recovery.

Like the cadets, the kidnapper was a few ranks back from the space cleared for the telepath. But he was close enough to take an energy weapon from his pocket and stun Perris as he walked by . . . or even kill him, if that was the scarred man's intent.

To that point, the kidnapper hadn't noticed the offworlders. He was too intent on the ceremonial route.

Mitchell turned in the direction of the Eastern Temple. He couldn't see the telepath—but from the reaction of the crowd, it seemed Perris was still a good couple of minutes away.

Kirk cursed. "There's another one."

The plebe looked at him, then at the crowd. "Where?"

The lieutenant pointed with his thumb, keeping it hidden between them. "Over there."

It took a moment, but Mitchell found the Heiren in question. He was one of the kidnappers they had found in the room with Perris.

"And there's another," Kirk rasped.

The underclassman found that one, too. By then, his heart had begun pumping like a jackhammer.

"What do we do?" he wondered. It wasn't a question so much as a way of ordering his thoughts.

The lieutenant answered it anyway. "We remain calm," he said. "We . . . Wait a second. What's he doing?"

Kirk was staring in the direction of the Heiren with the scar. It appeared the kidnapper was signaling to someone—but not, it seemed, to either of the accomplices the cadets had spotted. No, it was someone a good deal closer to the ceremonial route. . . .

Then Mitchell saw it—a Heiren returning the kidnapper's signal. But it wasn't just another person in the crowd.

It was one of Lenna's guards!

The man's red and white uniform was unmistakable. So was the eye contact he made with Scarface.

"Damn," said Kirk.

"You see it, too?" the plebe responded.

"I wish I didn't."

"That guard is in league with the dissidents. That complicates matters," Mitchell pointed out.

"Considerably," the lieutenant responded tightly, the muscles rippling in his jaw.

After all, their orders were to alert the nearest guard if they saw a problem developing. But if the nearest guard was in cahoots with the enemy, that didn't seem like a viable option.

"We've got to stop them," said Kirk.

Mitchell nodded. "And without causing too big a commotion. Otherwise, we'll just speed up their time-table."

"Or put a crimp in the reconciliation ceremony," the lieutenant observed, "and create an atmosphere of distrust."

"Which will serve the dissidents' purpose just as well," the plebe acknowledged. He shook his head in frustration.

They couldn't even transmit a call for help. Heiren custom had prohibited them from carrying communicators.

"Tell you what," Kirk said grimly. "I'll take the man with the scar and then the guard. You take the other two."

Mitchell nodded in agreement, knowing there was no time to argue about it. "And if we encounter some other problems along the way?"

The lieutenant looked as if he'd eaten something rotten. "We'll have to cross that bridge when we come to it."

"You're the boss," the plebe told him.

Then he started after the nearest kidnapper—and hoped desperately that he'd get there in time.

Chapter Nineteen

FORTUNATELY FOR KIRK, the Heiren with the scar was too intent on his objective to see the cadet circling around behind him. And when the kidnapper finally noticed that something might be amiss, it was too late for him to do anything about it.

Kirk's first blow caught the dissident just above the belt and to the right—where it would have struck a kidney if the kidnapper had been human. And certainly, that would have been bad enough.

But in a Heiren, that area housed an even more important organ—one that controlled the aeration of blood in the body. Hitting it was like hitting a human in the lungs; it momentarily stopped the supply of oxygen to the kidnapper's brain.

The effect was to stun the Heiren—to keep him off balance. The lieutenant's second blow was a hard chop to the nerve cluster at the base of the kidnapper's neck. Kirk saw the man's eyes roll back, a good indication that he had lost consciousness.

Had the crowd been packed less densely around the kidnapper, he would have fallen to the ground. As it was, his head lolled and he merely slumped against the celebrant beside him.

His work done for the moment, the lieutenant looked for Mitchell in the throng. He spotted the underclassman some thirty meters away, near the first of his assignments.

Like the scarred man, Mitchell's target looked to have been knocked senseless. And in his case, too, none of his neighbors seemed to have noticed that anything was wrong.

So far, so good, Kirk thought.

Then he turned in the direction of the ceremonial route. It was impossible to see Perris Nodarh yet, but he could tell from the crowd's excitement that the telepath was getting closer.

Unfortunately, there was no telling how long the traitorous guard would wait before making his move. Gritting his teeth, the lieutenant set out after him, forcing himself sideways between two burly onlookers.

"Where do you think you're going?" one of them asked, his yellow eyes slitting with undisguised annoyance.

"Yes, where?" asked the other Heiren. "Didn't your foster parents teach you any manners?"

Kirk understood the reference. Heir'tza traditionally gave their children to uncles and aunts to raise, believing that bloodparents were liable to coddle their offspring.

He didn't have time to explain that he hadn't been raised on this world, or that he was human and an officer in Starfleet, or even that the Heir'och telepath's life might be hanging in the balance. So rather than tender any answer at all, the lieutenant ignored the comments and continued to push his way through the crowd.

He incited additional antagonism along the way, but—in his own mind, at least—it seemed less and less important as he went on. Kirk was much more interested in Perris Nodarh, whom he could see every now and then over the heads of the intervening spectators.

The telepath was already within a hundred meters of the traitor. If the guard had wanted to, he could have taken out a weapon and cut Perris down right then and there. But he seemed content to wait.

More than likely, the lieutenant mused, the Heiren was worried about screwing up his assignment. And the closer his target got, the less chance there was that he would miss.

Suddenly, Kirk felt himself grabbed and spun around by a powerful pair of hands. He found himself looking into a scaly, bronze face and a pair of angry, yellow eyes.

"I've been standing here all day," the spectator complained. "Who are you to shove your way in front of me?"

The lieutenant didn't respond to the challenge—at least, not with words. Instead, he stepped on the

Heiren's foot as hard as he could, causing the fellow to forget about him for the moment.

Then, before he could be detained any longer, Kirk inserted himself between two other onlookers. He was making progress, he told himself—but was he making it quickly enough? Wiping sweat from his brow, he found yet another opening and wedged himself into it.

Darting a glance in the telepath's direction, the lieutenant saw that Perris had come within sixty meters of the traitor. He cursed and worked harder, driving himself forward with more urgency.

It was like trying to run through a raging surf. But despite it, Kirk made headway, using his legs to push and his hands to thrust unsuspecting spectators out of the way.

With the telepath fifty meters away, Kirk slid between two Heiren females. With the telepath forty meters away, he stumbled over someone's foot and nearly fell, but caught himself and plunged on. With the telepath thirty meters away, he nearly knocked a man over in his haste.

But it wasn't going to be enough. The lieutenant could see that with terrible clarity. No matter how hard he pushed himself, no matter how desperately he tried to breast the sea of onlookers, he wasn't closing with the guard as quickly as the telepath was.

Then the thing he feared, the thing he had been trying all along to prevent, came to pass. Before Kirk's horrified eyes, the traitor reached into his pocket and took out a directed-energy device.

No one else saw it because no one else was paying

attention to him. Everyone in the crowd was focused on Perris Nodarh, the remarkable telepath of Heir'-ocha, the hope of two worlds. With history unfolding before them, who even noticed a guard standing quietly along the ceremonial route, a weapon concealed in the palm of his hand?

Only Kirk.

He had to stop the traitor, just as he and Mitchell had stopped the other dissidents. But there were still four or five ranks of Heiren packed between the lieutenant and his objective. At this rate, it would take him a minute or more to get to the guard.

By that time, Perris Nodarh would be stretched out on the street and the ceremony would be in disarray. People would be screaming and running for cover and trampling their fellow Heiren in their confusion. Most important, the great reconciliation between the Hier'och and the Heir'tza would have died a stillborn death.

Kirk tried to shout a warning, tried to let some of the other guards know what was happening. But the crowd was too loud. He couldn't have made himself heard if he bellowed all day.

What are you going to do now? the lieutenant demanded of himself. *There's got to be something . . . there's always something. Isn't that what you teach your students? Isn't that what your professors taught you?*

Think about what others have done in similar situations. Construct parallels and analogies. Draw on the wisdom of your predecessors.

But which of his predecessors had ever found himself in a situation like this one? None that he knew of. Kirk was alone, abandoned by Starfleet history, left to his own resources.

As his mind raced, the telepath approached the traitor. Calmly, the man raised his weapon. Just as calmly, he prepared to fire.

What are you going to do? the lieutenant asked himself again. *How are you going to put an end to this madness?*

How?

Then, out of nowhere, a more pointed question occurred to him: What would *Mitchell* do?

Suddenly, Kirk moved.

He didn't think about it. He didn't consider the implications. He just grabbed the Heiren in front of him and pushed as hard as he could, and kept pushing until the man toppled into the fellow in front of him, who pitched into the spectator in front of *him* . . .

And so on and so on, down the line.

They went down like dominoes, one after the other, in an almost comical, ever-expanding wave. Just before it reached the traitor, he must have caught sight of something out of the corner of his eye, because he turned his head to have a look.

But he was too late. The falling dominoes had arrived at their ultimate destination—and that destination was him. As a tall, ungainly-looking Heiren fell heavily on the guard's legs, he cried out and went down in a heap . . . his weapon unfired.

Suddenly, with all those people lying on top of each

other in front of him, the lieutenant found he had a clear path to the traitor. Sprinting forward over the bodies of the fallen spectators, he saw the guard fumbling with his directed-energy device, trying to steady it and draw a bead on the startled Perris Nodarh.

Launching himself across the last onlooker in his way, Kirk came down on the traitor. One hand drove the Heiren's chin into the ground while the other reached for the weapon.

The guard was stunned and bloodied, but he didn't give the device up easily. What's more, he was stronger than he looked. For a moment, the lieutenant rolled and grappled with him, fighting for control of the Heiren's weapon. Then he got in a blow to his adversary's throat.

With the wind knocked out of him, the traitor's knees buckled and he let go of his energy device. By that time, another couple of guards had seen the disturbance and descended on them. Ignorant of the details, one of them pulled Kirk away while the other snatched the weapon from him.

"No," said a voice. "Not him. The *guard*."

The lieutenant looked around and saw that it was the telepath who had spoken. The guards glanced at their comrade, who was lying on the ground, gasping for breath. Then they turned to Kirk again.

It had to be hard for them to go against their instincts—no matter who had advised them to do so. The lieutenant watched their faces, trying to see which way they were leaning.

Michael Jan Friedman

"Let him go," Perris insisted.

Everyone who had been watching the telepath was now watching the guards, waiting to see what they would do. Would they comply with Perris Nodarh's instructions or defy them?

In the end, the Heir'tza had no choice—it was either follow the telepath's directions or take a chance on upsetting the ceremonial applecart. Frowning, they took their wayward comrade into custody.

As the lieutenant dusted himself off, he regarded Perris Nodarh. The fellow looked shaken by the close call—in a way, even more shaken than when the cadets had discovered him in the kidnappers' lair.

But as Kirk watched, the telepath composed himself. He found some inner focus, some place of calm in which to dwell.

Then he resumed his walk.

For a second or two, the crowds on both sides of the road were silent. But before long, a couple of Heiren began to clap for Perris Nodarh—not only for what he represented, but for his courage and determination in the face of what had obviously been an armed threat.

Little by little, others took up the applause, and it swept from one part of the throng to another—like wildfire in a field of dry corn, the lieutenant thought. The telepath acknowledged it with a wave or two, and the crowd roared its approval even louder.

The Heiren loved him, down to the last man, woman, and child—and at that moment, they would have done anything to show it. It was a wondrous thing for an offworlder to behold.

244

In fact, Kirk was starting to get caught up in the euphoria himself. Despite his tendency to anticipate trouble, he was beginning to get the feeling the rest of the ceremony might go more smoothly.

"Man," said a voice behind him. "For a second or two, I thought we were in trouble there."

The lieutenant didn't have to turn around to know it was Mitchell who had made the comment. He smiled to himself.

"No trouble at all," Kirk told his fellow cadet. "One just has to be up to the challenge."

Mitchell grunted. "Uh-huh. Or lucky."

The lieutenant considered the notion for a moment. "Or lucky," he was forced to concede.

Gary Mitchell had never been in a parade before.

Back home, in New York City, there had been a parade almost every Sunday to celebrate one thing or another. But he had always been a spectator—on the outside, looking in.

That day, on an alien planet several light-years from Earth, it was different. For once in his life, the underclassman from the Big City was on the inside looking out.

Of course, neither he nor Kirk wanted to attract any attention, so they strolled along the edge of the road rather than the middle. Also, they made sure to hang back a good twenty meters from Perris Nodarh.

After all, the Heiren of two worlds hadn't gathered there in the thousands to see a couple of tired, sweaty Starfleet cadets. They wanted a glimpse of the telepaths who held their species' hopes in their hands, and Mitchell and his friend were only too happy to remain in the background.

Only Minister Lenna's guards paid any real attention to them—and it was all good. Like visiting dignitaries, they nodded to each white-and-red figure they passed and received a nod in return.

More than once along the route, Mitchell and Kirk told each other they were providing extra security for Perris. But truthfully, the plebe just wanted to be there to see the telepath meet his Heir'tza counterpart in Heir'at's central edifice, which was looming ahead of them in all its open-arched, bronze-roofed glory. And despite Kirk's protests to the contrary, it was obvious he was intent on the same thing.

As luck would have it, there were no other incidents of violence. There wasn't even a hint of one. In a matter of a few minutes, the Heir'och telepath reached his destination.

He walked up a handful of broad, shallow steps, entered the ancient Government House on his bare feet and approached the building's open-air ceremonial hall. At the same time, another figure approached from the west—a female Heiren in a white robe trimmed with red.

The other telepath, Mitchell thought.

She was slender, petite . . . little more than a child, he realized. And yet her people, the Heir'tza, had seen fit to place a great responsibility on her narrow shoulders.

The cadet hoped they had made the right decision.

As the telepaths caught sight of one another, they smiled. Obviously, neither of them had ever done this sort of thing before—and now that they were faced with it, they seemed to feel a little self-conscious.

There were other Heiren present in the hall as well—leaders and luminaries representing the Heir'-och and the Heir'tza, dressed in the somber robes of their offices. But Mitchell didn't really dwell on them, and it seemed to him no one else did either.

It was the telepaths whom people cared about. For good or ill, they were the ones who would determine the future of their species—the ones who would chart their society's course for decades to come.

Perris and his opposite number seemed to collect themselves for a moment or two. Then they moved a step closer to each other and gazed deeply into each other's eyes.

Mitchell found he was holding his breath. Everyone was, he realized, Heir'och and Heir'tza alike. And they continued to hold their breath for what seemed like a very long time.

On a plane the cadet couldn't hope to approach, intuition or no intuition, the telepaths were exchanging promises. They were warranting the intentions of their respective peoples and their respective leaders. They were offering assurances, making pledges, furnishing guarantees . . . and they were doing it in the only language that really meant anything to either of them.

The language of their minds.

Mitchell couldn't "hear" what was passing between Perris and the girl. But by watching their expressions, by opening himself up to them, he could sense the tone of their conversation. To his delight, it was more than cordial. It was as if the telepaths were old friends.

"It's working," he found himself saying.

Kirk turned to him. "How do you—?" And then he caught himself. "What I mean is . . . that's good to hear."

As the cadets looked on, the telepaths smiled again. But this time, it wasn't an expression of embarrassment or self-consciousness. It was a display of elation and accomplishment, the magnitude of which neither of them had known before.

They weren't the only ones who witnessed it, either. The Heiren masses who had gathered around the government building saw the looks on the telepaths' faces and cheered, and the cheer spread out in concentric circles like the echo of a stone dropped in a pool of still water.

In seconds, the cheer had filled the streets surrounding the building. In a few more, it had gone beyond that. And as far as Mitchell could tell, it kept going undiminished—a wave that seemed destined to run through the entire city, stretching as far as its most distant precincts.

Despite the kidnappers' best efforts, the telepaths had achieved all they had set out to do. Peace and unity had been secured. With luck, the Heiren would enjoy a different society from that point on.

Kirk turned to the underclassman. "All's well that ends well, eh?"

Mitchell nodded. "I suppose."

The lieutenant continued to look at him. "You know," he said, "I owe you some kind of apology."

"Oh?" said the plebe.

"I was selfish," Kirk admitted. "I thought my career was the most important thing in the galaxy."

"And?" asked Mitchell.

"And it's not."

"Hell," the underclassman responded cheerfully, "I could have told you that. All you had to do was ask."

Kirk scowled at him. "I'm trying to apologize, dammit."

"And I'm trying to accept," Mitchell responded.

The lieutenant sighed heavily. "You're never going to let me forget this, are you?"

"Never," the plebe confirmed.

"Uh-oh," said Kirk, his eyes locking on something in the distance.

"What is it?" asked Mitchell, following his friend's gaze and expecting to see him point out another threat.

"This isn't good," Kirk told him. "Not at all."

"What isn't?" The underclassman insisted on an answer, his heart racing with anticipation.

The lieutenant tilted his head to one side and uttered a single, chilling word: "Bannock."

Mitchell looked at him. "Bannock?"

"Bannock," Kirk confirmed.

The underclassman took a breath of relief—not that the captain's presence there was a blessing, exactly, but it wasn't quite the menace he had anticipated. "Where is he?"

"Just outside the government building," the lieutenant told him. "On the other side."

A moment later, the underclassman found Bannock

among the dignitaries amassed near the telepaths. Unfortunately, the captain seemed to have found them as well. He was glaring directly at the cadets, his eyes a startling blue in the bright afternoon light.

"He sees us," said Mitchell.

"Tell me about it."

"And we're not at the bakery," the plebe pointed out.

"We're very much not at the bakery," Kirk replied.

"We're in trouble," said Mitchell, "aren't we?"

The lieutenant grunted. "Has anyone ever told you what a talent you have for understatement?"

Under normal circumstances, the underclassman would have come up with a ridiculously clever quip in response. But under these circumstances, he didn't much feel like it.

Chapter Twenty

KIRK MADE SURE to arrive at the *Republic*'s briefing room a few minutes earlier than necessary. He also made sure his friend Mitchell arrived there alongside him.

Entering the room, the cadets took their places at one end of it. Then they locked their hands behind their backs, took a couple of deep breaths, and awaited their fate.

As he stood there, the lieutenant couldn't help but recall the captain's instructions. Unfortunately, they were rather explicit. In fact, if memory served, he had issued them twice.

Under no circumstances whatsoever are you to leave the vicinity of the bakery.

No circumstances, Bannock had told them. Whatsoever. It didn't leave much room for interpretation, did it?

"What are you thinking?" asked Mitchell.

"I'm thinking I'd rather be facing a room full of Heiren kidnappers than be standing here waiting for Captain Bannock." After a moment, Kirk decided that wasn't quite right. "Make that a room full of *Klingon* kidnappers . . . all of them in a bad mood. A *very* bad mood."

The underclassman nodded. "I feel the same way, pal. But, listen . . . what's done is done. Whatever happens now is in the lap of the gods."

The lieutenant turned to his friend. "In the what?"

Mitchell shrugged. "You know, the lap of the gods. The hands of Fate. *Que será, será* and all that business."

"It's beyond our control, you're saying?"

"Beyond our control," the plebe confirmed. "Exactly."

"So there's no need to worry," the lieutenant concluded.

"That's right."

Kirk grunted. "But I am worried."

"But you shouldn't be," Mitchell argued.

"But I *am,*" the upperclassman insisted.

He would never know if his friend had a response for that, because the door chose that moment to slide aside with a soft whoosh. A moment later, Bannock entered the room.

With an icy glance at Mitchell and Kirk, he sat down. Then he leaned back in his chair, folded his arms across his chest and studied the cadets, his own face expressionless and unreadable.

Kirk waited for the captain to say something. But he didn't. He just stared at them. Finally, the man cleared his throat, signaling that he was about to speak after all.

"Do you know what you did today?" Bannock asked them, his voice so calm it was almost eerie.

Kirk started to provide him with a summary.

"No," Bannock insisted, holding his hand up for silence. "Don't tell me. I'll tell you."

The lieutenant swallowed. This didn't sound good. He watched as the captain ticked off item number one on his leathery fingers.

"First," said Bannock, "by using directed-energy weapons within the boundaries of Heir'at, you violated one of the oldest and most sacred laws of an alien culture."

There was no arguing with that. First Minister Lenna had forgiven the cadets their indiscretion, of course, but they hadn't known in advance that the minister would be so generous.

"Second," the captain continued, ticking off finger number two, "you knowingly and intentionally ignored my orders by leaving the vicinity of the bakery and proceeding on your own."

Kirk winced. True also, he thought, though he had hoped for a little leeway in the matter.

"Finally," said Bannock, ticking off finger number three, "as if all that weren't enough, you put the populations of two entire planets at risk with your bullheaded and ill-considered derring-do."

The lieutenant could see his Starfleet career taking wing. *Maybe I can get a job on a freighter,* he mused. *Or a passenger transport. It's not what I had hoped for, but at least I'll be out in space.*

Kirk thought about Captain April and Admiral Mallory. He thought about how they had gone to bat for him, and how he had ultimately let them down. That was the worst part for him, by far—the knowledge that he hadn't been worthy of the trust they had placed in him.

"All in all," Bannock concluded, "I'd say the two of you had a busy day. If it had lasted a little longer, maybe you could also have started another shooting war with the Romulans and radioed our ship designs to the Klingon High Council."

The lieutenant didn't respond. He didn't offer any excuses either. After all, they wouldn't have done him or his friend any good. He just kept his chin up and consoled himself with the knowledge that the captain's speech couldn't go on much longer.

But Mitchell didn't seem capable of exercising the same restraint. "Permission to speak freely, sir," he said.

Bannock considered him. "Permission denied."

"But, sir," the plebe persisted, "none of what happened down there was Jim's fault. I—"

"Enough," the captain growled.

"But, sir—"

"But *nothing,* Mr. Mitchell."

Bannock leaned forward in his seat. His eyes looked as if they would spit fire at the underclassman.

"You're equally to blame," the captain said. "Equally in the wrong."

Mitchell's nostrils flared and his mouth became a taut, white line, but he finally stopped arguing. Apparently, thought Kirk, even the plebe had seen that it was futile to say anything at that point.

Still, Bannock wasn't finished yet. "The two of you demonstrated an inability to follow orders, a marked lack of respect for other cultures' mores, and an overeagerness to take foolhardy risks. In case you were wondering, those aren't qualities we cherish in Starfleet." He turned to the lieutenant. "Are they, Mr. Kirk?"

The upperclassman couldn't help frowning. "No, sir," he answered reluctantly, "they're not."

"And it wouldn't be unreasonable of me to have you both booted out of the Academy for this . . . would it?"

Kirk swallowed. "No, sir," he answered again.

Bannock's face darkened. "Especially when you consider what happened in the sensor room the other night. In light of that, it would be anything *but* unreasonable to relieve the Academy of your presence—and clear the way for men and women who can obey a simple order. Isn't that true, Lieutenant?"

Kirk eyed him. "Yes, sir," he said quietly, "it is."

The captain leaned back in his chair again. Finally, the lieutenant thought, their ordeal was over. He and his friend could slink back to their quarters and try to piece together the rest of their lives.

Suddenly, the captain did the last thing Kirk would have expected of him. He *smiled.*

Michael Jan Friedman

"On the other hand," Bannock observed in an almost congenial tone, "it would've been difficult for anyone—me included—to stand by and watch that telepath get abducted."

The lieutenant wasn't sure he had heard correctly. "Sir?"

"Aren't you paying attention, Mr. Kirk? I said I couldn't have stood there and watched them kidnap the telepath either."

"Yes, sir," the upperclassman replied warily, wondering if the captain was playing some kind of game with them.

"So you *are* listening," said Bannock. "That's good, Lieutenant." He stroked his chin. "Considering the serious nature of the situation and the favorable results you achieved, however the means, it would be the height of foolishness for me to bring charges against you. Instead, I'm going to file a commendation saying you displayed outstanding initiative, courage, and cleverness in the face of great odds."

Kirk was feeling a little dizzy. "We did?"

"Of *course* we did," said Mitchell, casting a sidelong glance at him.

The lieutenant recovered as best he could. "Uh . . . Yes, sir."

"If not for you two," the captain noted, "the Heiren factions might never have been reunited. Both Heir'ocha and Heir'tza owe you a debt of gratitude. And as for me . . . I'm proud of you. Proud of *both* of you." He turned to the underclassman, a surprisingly mischievous gleam in his eye. "That means you, too, Mr. Mitchell."

The plebe smiled a rakish smile. "Why, thank you, sir. I'm glad we had the opportunity to be of service."

Bannock harrumphed. "Don't push it, Cadet."

Mitchell straightened. "Don't worry, sir, I won't."

"Good." The man's eyes narrowed. "You know, I may have been too quick to frown on a little insubordination. After what you showed me on Heir'tza, I'm going to have to consider it in a new light."

The captain looked at Kirk as if he expected some kind of response. The lieutenant wasn't sure what to say.

"That was a joke, son," said Bannock. He turned to the other cadet. "Wasn't it, Mr. Mitchell?"

Mitchell's smile widened. "It certainly was, sir."

"You know," the captain told him, his voice taking on a confidential tone, "I don't know what to do with Lieutenant Kirk sometimes. The man doesn't have much of a sense of humor."

"No, sir," said the underclassman, "he doesn't. But if you like, I could help him along in that regard."

Bannock turned to Kirk and nodded approvingly. "Yes," he said, "I believe I would like that. That is, if you think he's salvageable."

"I do, sir."

"In that case," the captain told him, "give it your best shot. Consider that an order."

The lieutenant sighed. "Begging your pardon, Captain, but do I have a say in this?"

Bannock turned to him and shook his head emphatically from side to side. "You most certainly do not."

Kirk bit his lip. He had liked it better when Mitchell and the captain were at odds with each other.

"Well, then," said the captain, "I guess we're done here." He got up from his seat, pulled down on his uniform shirt, and said, "Dismissed, gentlemen." Then, with a chuckle to himself, he left the briefing room.

Mitchell turned to the upperclassman. "You see? Even Bannock thinks you need to loosen up."

"Don't start," Kirk warned him.

"Don't they tell jokes back in Iowa? Too much corn in their diets, maybe? Or do you think it's a genetic problem?"

The lieutenant shot him a look of warning. "I said don't *start . . .*"

Mitchell didn't see Kirk the rest of that day.

The underclassman spent the better part of it in engineering, learning some tricks of the trade from Chief Hogan. The lieutenant, on the other hand, passed the time ensconced in his favorite place—behind the helm controls of the *Republic*.

But that evening, at dinnertime, the cadets were reunited. Mitchell walked into the mess hall and saw Kirk sitting there—at a table all by himself, just like at the Academy.

The plebe wondered why that would be. After all, the man had friends here, Bannock among them. There was no reason why he should be eating alone. Grabbing a tray and some vaguely edible-looking Italian food, Mitchell went to join his fellow cadet.

Noting his approach, the lieutenant looked up from his meal. He didn't seem happy in the least.

"What is it?" asked the underclassman, sitting down opposite Kirk.

The lieutenant shook his head. "Nothing."

"You're sure?" asked Mitchell.

"I'm sure," said Kirk. He aimlessly moved some spaghetti bolognese around his plate. "Incidentally," he remarked, "I went to have another talk with Captain Bannock."

Mitchell was interested. "What about?"

"I wanted to know why he put us on the same team on Heir'tza, considering he had promised to drive a wedge between us."

"And?" asked the plebe.

"When I got to his quarters, he was speaking with some of the Heiren leaders." The lieutenant grunted. "You'll be happy to know everything's going swimmingly on Heir'tza. The telepaths are doing a great job and the reconciliation is well under way. Oh . . . and Ar Bintor survived those kidnappers. He's resting now in a Heir'at medical facility."

Mitchell nodded. "That's good. I mean, it's terrific, it's wonderful. But what did Bannock say?" he asked, his curiosity aroused. "You know, about putting us together?"

Kirk twirled some pasta around his fork. "He said he wanted to test my resolve. He wanted to make sure I could resist your evil influences even when we were working shoulder to shoulder."

It made sense, the plebe supposed. "And, of course, he wasn't expecting any real trouble."

259

"Uh-huh. So it was a perfect time to conduct his experiment."

"Which you failed, of course," Mitchell observed.

"With flying colors," the lieutenant responded.

He smiled—but only for a moment. Then he seemed to remember something and he turned somber again.

"You know," said Mitchell, "you're doing a good impersonation of that freezer unit again."

"I know," Kirk conceded.

"The captain wouldn't like that," the underclassman reminded him.

"No," the lieutenant admitted, "I don't suppose he would." But that, it seemed, was all he cared to say on the subject.

Mitchell shrugged. "Suit yourself. But if you were to loosen up, I bet it would do wonders for your relationship with Phelana."

The lieutenant winced.

"What?" asked the plebe, needing no flashes of intuition to realize he had hit a sore spot.

"I broke up with her," Kirk told him bluntly.

Suddenly, Mitchell understood his friend's malaise. "What made you do that?" he wondered.

The lieutenant shrugged. "I had to."

"Had to?" the underclassman echoed.

Kirk nodded. "She wouldn't make the jump."

Mitchell was about to ask what his friend meant by that—and then he figured it out. There had been a bond between the lieutenant and Phelana—a recognition that they approached life the same way, with the same degree of purpose and determination. When the

Andorian informed Kirk that he had to jump off that roof without her, she was really admitting that that bond was no longer valid.

The lieutenant sighed as he maneuvered his food around some more. "I thought Phelana was special."

"They're all special," Mitchell told him. "All amazing creatures, each of them in her own way. But that's the beauty of it, isn't it?"

"What is?" Kirk asked him.

The plebe leaned forward. "Just when you think the perfect woman has dropped out of your life forever, an even more perfect woman shows up to take her place."

The upperclassman glanced at him. "Maybe it works that way for you."

"It can work that way for you, too, pal," Mitchell assured him.

Kirk turned to him. "Meaning?"

The plebe shrugged playfully. "Meaning your old buddy Gary doesn't let any grass grow under his feet. Back at the Academy, when you were telling me you absolutely, positively didn't want me to set you up with a date . . . well, I happened to run into this first-year engineering student—this very attractive first-year engineering student—with the biggest baby blue eyes and the most incredible laugh . . ."

"Oh, no, you don't," said the lieutenant.

"She'd be perfect for you," Mitchell insisted.

Kirk shook his head. "I can't let myself get involved with someone else now. It's too soon."

The underclassman stared at him. "Too soon . . . ? Come on, Jim. Phelana's not dead, she's just—"

261

"You say . . . she's attractive?" the lieutenant asked abruptly.

Mitchell was surprised. "Uh, yeah. Very attractive."

"And . . . what kind of laugh . . . ?"

"An incredible laugh," the plebe told him. "But, really, I think you should hear it in person and judge for yourself."

Kirk's eyes fixed on infinity as he considered the prospect. "You know, maybe I should, at that."

"You mean just as soon as you get over Phelana."

His friend snapped out of his reverie. "Right," he said. "As soon as I get over Phelana."

Mitchell laughed. Then he reached across the table and clapped his friend on the shoulder.

"What?" asked the lieutenant.

"Nothing," said the plebe. "Just eat your spaghetti."

Jim Kirk was still a project, Mitchell mused. He still had a long way to go, a lot of rough edges to smooth over before he was done. But the man was starting to show signs of promise.

"Come on," the underclassman said. "Finish up, already. I want to see if we can get into some *real* trouble."

Chapter Twenty-one

KIRK TURNED TO SPOCK, his memories of Gary and the *Republic* already fading in his mind's eye. He sat back heavily in his chair, feeling the weight of the intervening years.

"And that was it," he said. "We completed our survey mission and returned to Earth, where we resumed our studies."

Of course, the captain had "cleaned up" the story a little to accommodate the Vulcan's sense of propriety, and left things out that were nobody's business but his own. Outside of that, however, he had related it pretty much as he remembered it.

"You were friends again," Spock observed.

"Yes," said Kirk. "Better friends than before, in fact."

The Vulcan nodded. "Fascinating."

The captain looked at him askance. "You mean that, Spock? Or are you just saying it to be polite?"

"My comment was sincere," the other man assured him. "I was genuinely intrigued by your tale."

"And why is that?" Kirk wondered.

The Vulcan shrugged. "Lieutenant Mitchell had a significantly greater influence on you than I would have imagined."

"Influence?" the captain echoed. "You mean in terms of 'loosening me up,' as Gary put it?"

"No," said Spock, raising an eyebrow. "I'm referring to something else entirely. Prior to meeting Lieutenant Mitchell, it seems you were rather conservative in your choice of strategies. It was he, apparently, who showed you the value of taking risks."

"Showed me . . . ?" Kirk began. He dismissed the idea with a wave of his hand. "Believe me, Spock, it wasn't that way at all."

"Your account would seem to indicate otherwise," the Vulcan replied matter-of-factly.

The captain chuckled. "Despite what Gary may have said, I took lots of chances before I met him. Too many to count."

The first officer regarded him. "For example?"

Kirk thought about it for thirty seconds or more. Surprisingly, nothing leaped out at him.

"All right," he said. "Maybe I can't come up with an example on the spur of the moment. But that doesn't mean there weren't plenty of times I leaped before I looked."

Still, even as the captain uttered the words, he

began to wonder . . . was there a seed of truth in what Spock was saying? Was Gary the one who had taught him to take chances?

He had been tap-dancing for so long, bluffing with the best of them, it was difficult for him to see himself any other way. But maybe . . . just maybe . . . his first officer had a point.

"Perhaps you are right," Spock responded. "It is difficult for me to say, not having been present at the time. In any case, it was merely an observation, of no real practical importance. If I were you, I would not concern myself with it."

In other words, Kirk thought, the Vulcan was letting him off the hook. He felt a pang of gratitude.

Spock's brow crinkled. "I have a question, sir. The order imposed on the cadets that night on the *Republic* . . . ?"

"When Commander Mangione confined us to our quarters?"

"Yes," the Vulcan confirmed. "Did you make any further attempts to discover the reason for the restriction?"

Kirk shook his head. "I didn't. I was certain that whatever happened that night would remain Starfleet's little secret. In fact, I was told at one point that no one under the rank of admiral could access the file."

"I see," said the first officer. "In that case, you must have been surprised when you *did* find out."

"Didn't I *look* surprised?" the captain asked.

Spock thought back to the events of a few months

earlier. "It was difficult to tell at the time," he decided. "I still have trouble deciphering human expressions."

Kirk smiled. "Then trust me—I was surprised, all right. I was very surprised."

The Vulcan nodded. Then he unfolded his slender frame and got up from his chair. "I should return to the bridge."

The captain nodded. "I'll be up there soon enough myself."

Spock turned to go. But before he reached the door, Kirk made a point of clearing his throat.

The first officer looked back at him. "Yes, sir?"

The captain shrugged. "Thanks."

Spock tilted his head. "For . . . ?"

"For listening," Kirk told him. He smiled. "That's all, really. Just for listening."

The Vulcan seemed to understand. What's more, the captain gathered, Spock appeared to take some pride in his contribution.

"You are welcome," he said.

Then the first officer departed Kirk's quarters, leaving the captain all by himself. But it was all right for him to be alone now. He felt better having told Spock his story.

Turning to his monitor, he took a deep breath. Then he opened a new file and began entering some notes. After all, Kelso's funeral would take place in a few hours, and he wanted to do the man justice.

"Captain?" came a voice.

Responding to his communications officer, Kirk glanced at the ceiling. "Yes, Mr. Dezago?"

"You have a message, sir. From Earth."

The captain had a feeling he knew who it was from. He felt a shadow fall over him.

"Put it through," he told Dezago.

"Aye, sir," said the officer.

A moment later, Kirk's monitor showed him the face of Gary's father. Thomas Mitchell was a broad, powerful-looking man with thinning gray hair and his son's dark eyes. His face was hollow-cheeked with grief, making him look old beyond his years.

"We got the news this morning, Jim. Naturally, we're . . ." His voice caught and cracked. "We're devastated," he said. "But then, I'm sure you are, too. Nobody was closer to Gary than you were."

The captain felt a lump in his throat. He tried to swallow it away, but it wouldn't budge.

"We're going to hold the funeral here in New York," Gary's father went on doggedly. "A week from to-day—that's Tuesday. I know you'll want to attend. And if you don't mind . . ." Again, Thomas Mitchell seemed to find himself stricken speechless for a moment. "If you don't mind, Jim, we'd like you to deliver the eulogy."

Kirk nodded. "Of course," he said out loud, as if Gary's father could hear him across the light-years that separated them. "Of course."

It was the least he could do . . . considering he was the man who had killed Thomas Mitchell's son.

Look for STAR TREK Fiction from Pocket Books

Star Trek®: The Original Series

Star Trek: The Motion Picture • Gene Roddenberry
Star Trek II: The Wrath of Khan • Vonda N. McIntyre
Star Trek III: The Search for Spock • Vonda N. McIntyre
Star Trek IV: The Voyage Home • Vonda N. McIntyre
Star Trek V: The Final Frontier • J. M. Dillard
Star Trek VI: The Undiscovered Country • J. M. Dillard
Star Trek VII: Generations • J. M. Dillard
Enterprise: The First Adventure • Vonda N. McIntyre
Final Frontier • Diane Carey
Strangers from the Sky • Margaret Wander Bonanno
Spock's World • Diane Duane
The Lost Years • J. M. Dillard
Probe • Margaret Wander Bonanno
Prime Directive • Judith and Garfield Reeves-Stevens
Best Destiny • Diane Carey
Shadows on the Sun • Michael Jan Friedman
Sarek • A. C. Crispin
Federation • Judith and Garfield Reeves-Stevens
The Ashes of Eden • William Shatner & Judith and Garfield
    Reeves-Stevens
The Return • William Shatner & Judith and Garfield Reeves-
    Stevens
Star Trek: Starfleet Academy • Diane Carey
Vulcan's Forge • Josepha Sherman and Susan Shwartz
Avenger • William Shatner & Judith and Garfield Reeves-Stevens

#1 *Star Trek: The Motion Picture* • Gene Roddenberry
#2 *The Entropy Effect* • Vonda N. McIntyre
#3 *The Klingon Gambit* • Robert E. Vardeman
#4 *The Covenant of the Crown* • Howard Weinstein
#5 *The Prometheus Design* • Sondra Marshak & Myrna
    Culbreath
#6 *The Abode of Life* • Lee Correy
#7 *Star Trek II: The Wrath of Khan* • Vonda N. McIntyre
#8 *Black Fire* • Sonni Cooper
#9 *Triangle* • Sondra Marshak & Myrna Culbreath
#10 *Web of the Romulans* • M. S. Murdock
#11 *Yesterday's Son* • A. C. Crispin

Star Trek: The Next Generation®

Encounter at Farpoint • David Gerrold
Unification • Jeri Taylor
Relics • Michael Jan Friedman
Descent • Diane Carey
All Good Things • Michael Jan Friedman
Star Trek: Klingon • Dean W. Smith & Kristine K. Rusch
Star Trek VII: Generations • J. M. Dillard
Metamorphosis • Jean Lorrah
Vendetta • Peter David
Reunion • Michael Jan Friedman
Imzadi • Peter David
The Devil's Heart • Carmen Carter
Dark Mirror • Diane Duane
Q-Squared • Peter David
Crossover • Michael Jan Friedman
Kahless • Michael Jan Friedman
Star Trek: First Contact • J. M. Dillard
The Best and the Brightest • Susan Wright
Planet X • Jan Friedman

#1 *Ghost Ship* • Diane Carey
#2 *The Peacekeepers* • Gene DeWeese
#3 *The Children of Hamlin* • Carmen Carter
#4 *Survivors* • Jean Lorrah
#5 *Strike Zone* • Peter David
#6 *Power Hungry* • Howard Weinstein
#7 *Masks* • John Vornholt
#8 *The Captains' Honor* • David and Daniel Dvorkin
#9 *A Call to Darkness* • Michael Jan Friedman
#10 *A Rock and a Hard Place* • Peter David
#11 *Gulliver's Fugitives* • Keith Sharee
#12 *Doomsday World* • David, Carter, Friedman & Greenberg
#13 *The Eyes of the Beholders* • A. C. Crispin
#14 *Exiles* • Howard Weinstein
#15 *Fortune's Light* • Michael Jan Friedman
#16 *Contamination* • John Vornholt
#17 *Boogeymen* • Mel Gilden
#18 *Q-in-Law* • Peter David
#19 *Perchance to Dream* • Howard Weinstein

Star Trek: Deep Space Nine®

The Search • Diane Carey
Warped • K. W. Jeter
The Way of the Warrior • Diane Carey
Star Trek: Klingon • Dean W. Smith & Kristine K. Rusch
Trials and Tribble-ations • Diane Carey
Far Beyond the Stars • Steve Barnes

Star Trek®: Voyager™

Flashback • Diane Carey
Mosaic • Jeri Taylor

#1 *Caretaker* • L. A. Graf
#2 *The Escape* • Dean W. Smith & Kristine K. Rusch
#3 *Ragnarok* • Nathan Archer
#4 *Violations* • Susan Wright
#5 *Incident at Arbuk* • John Gregory Betancourt
#6 *The Murdered Sun* • Christie Golden
#7 *Ghost of a Chance* • Mark A. Garland & Charles G. McGraw
#8 *Cybersong* • S. N. Lewitt
#9 *Invasion #4: The Final Fury* • Dafydd ab Hugh
#10 *Bless the Beasts* • Karen Haber
#11 *The Garden* • Melissa Scott
#12 *Chrysalis* • David Niall Wilson
#13 *The Black Shore* • Greg Cox
#14 *Marooned* • Christie Golden
#15 *Echoes* • Dean W. Smith & Kristine K. Rusch
#16 *Seven of Nine* • Christie Golden

Star Trek®: New Frontier

#1 *House of Cards* • Peter David
#2 *Into the Void* • Peter David
#3 *The Two-Front War* • Peter David
#4 *End Game* • Peter David
#5 *Martyr* • Peter David
#6 *Fire on High* • Peter David

Star Trek®: Day of Honor

Book One: *Ancient Blood* • Diane Carey
Book Two: *Armageddon Sky* • L. A. Graf
Book Three: *Her Klingon Soul* • Michael Jan Friedman
Book Four: *Treaty's Law* • Dean W. Smith & Kristine K. Rusch

Star Trek®: The Captain's Table

Book One: *War Dragons* • L. A. Graf
Book Two: *Dujonian's Hoard* • Michael Jan Friedman
Book Three: *The Mist* • Dean W. Smith & Kristine K. Rusch
Book Four: *Fire Ship* • Diane Carey
Book Five: *Once Burned* • Peter David
Book Six: *Where Sea Meets Sky* • Jerry Oltion

Star Trek®: The Dominion War

Book One: *Behind Enemy Lines* • John Vornholt
Book Two: *Call to Arms . . .* • Diane Carey
Book Three: *Tunnel Through the Stars* • John Vornholt
Book Four: *. . . Sacrifice of Angels* • Diane Carey